Climb into this basketful of stories and you will find . . . a smelly giant, a man who rides on the back of a tiger, a wolf that tells riddles, a witch, a cat who likes playing the violin, and many other strange and exciting people and animals.

No story has been put in the basket without very careful inspection by children's book specialist Pat Thomson. All the stories are tried and tested favourites, and all by top children's authors – Margaret Mahy, Ted Hughes, Catherine Storr, Penelope Lively, Robin Klein, Russell Hoban and many others.

You won't want to stop reading until you get right to the bottom of the basket!

PAT THOMSON is a well-known author and anthologist. Additionally, she works as a lecturer and librarian in a teacher training college – work which involves a constant search for short stories which have both quality and child-appeal. She is also an Honorary Vice-President of the Federation of Children's Book Groups. She is married with two grown-up children and lives in Northamptonshire.

Also available by Pat Thomson,
and published by Doubleday and Corgi Books:

A BAND OF JOINING-IN STORIES

A BUS FULL OF STORIES FOR FOUR YEAR OLDS

A POCKETFUL OF STORIES FOR FIVE YEAR OLDS

A BUCKETFUL OF STORIES FOR SIX YEAR OLDS

A BOX OF STORIES FOR SIX YEAR OLDS

A BARREL OF STORIES FOR SEVEN YEAR OLDS

A SACKFUL OF STORIES FOR EIGHT YEAR OLDS

A CRATE OF STORIES FOR EIGHT YEAR OLDS

A CHEST OF STORIES FOR NINE YEAR OLDS

A SATCHEL OF SCHOOL STORIES

A BASKET
of Stories for
Seven Year Olds

COLLECTED BY PAT THOMSON

Illustrated by Rachel Birkett

CORGI BOOKS

A BASKET OF STORIES FOR SEVEN YEAR OLDS
A CORGI BOOK : 0 552 52729 7

First published in Great Britain by Doubleday,
a division of Transworld Publishers Ltd

PRINTING HISTORY
Doubleday edition published 1990
Corgi edition published 1992
Corgi edition reprinted 1993 (four times), 1994, 1995 (twice), 1996 (twice), 1998

Corgi Books are published by Transworld Publishers Ltd,
61–63 Uxbridge Road, Ealing, London W5 5SA,
in Australia by Transworld Publishers (Australia) Pty Ltd,
15–25 Helles Avenue, Moorebank, NSW 2170
and in New Zealand by Transworld Publishers (NZ) Ltd,
3 William Pickering Drive, Albany, Auckland.

Printed and bound in Great Britain by
Cox & Wyman Ltd, Reading, Berkshire.

Acknowledgements

The editor and publisher are grateful for permission to include the following copyright stories.

Leila Berg, 'The Man Who Rode the Tiger' from *Folk Tales*. Reprinted by permission of Hodder & Stoughton Ltd.

John Cunliffe, 'The Story of Giant Kippernose' from *Giant Kippernose and Other Stories*. Reprinted by permission of André Deutsch Ltd.

Dorothy Edwards, 'The Magician Who Kept a Pub' from *The Magician Who Kept a Pub* (Kestrel Books, 1975), copyright © Dorothy Edwards, 1975. Reprinted by permission of Penguin Books Ltd.

Russell Hoban, 'The Tin Horseman' from *La Corona and the Tin Frog* (Cape). Reprinted by permission of David Higham Associates Ltd.

Ted Hughes, 'How the Cat Became' from *How the Whale Became and Other Stories*. Reprinted by permission of Faber & Faber Ltd.

Robin Klein, 'J. Roodie' from *Ratbags and Rascals*. Reprinted by permission of P.I.X.E.L Publishing, Australia.

Penelope Lively, 'Uninvited Ghosts' from *Uninvited Ghosts* (William Heinemann Ltd 1984). Text copyright © Penelope Lively 1974, 1977, 1981, 1984. Reprinted with permission.

Margaret Mahy, 'Aunt Nasty' from *The Third Margaret Mahy Story Book*. Reprinted by permission of J M Dent & Sons Ltd.

Alf Prøysen, 'Mr Pepperpot Buys Macaroni' from *Little Old Mrs Pepperpot*. Reprinted by permission of Random Century Ltd.

James Reeves, 'Odysseus and Circe' from *Heroes and Monsters*, © James Reeves Estate. Reprinted by kind permission of The James Reeves Estate.

Catherine Storr, 'The Riddlemaster' from *The Adventures of Polly and the Wolf*. Reprinted by permission of Faber & Faber Ltd.

David Henry Wilson, 'Campers' from *How to Stop a Train with One Finger*. Reprinted by permission of J M Dent & Sons Ltd.

Sylvia Woods, 'Charlie Works a Miracle' from *Now Then Charlie Robinson*. Reprinted by permission of Faber & Faber Ltd.

CONTENTS

A BASKET OF STORIES
FOR SEVEN YEAR OLDS

The Story of Giant Kippernose

Once there was a giant called Kippernose. He lived on a lonely farm in the mountains. He was not fierce. Indeed he was as kind and as gentle as a giant could be. He liked children, and was fond of animals. He was good at telling stories. His favourite foods were ice-cream, cakes, lollipops and sausages. He would help anyone, large or small. And yet he had no friends. When he went to the town to do his shopping, everyone ran away from him. Busy streets emptied in a trice. Everyone ran home, bolted their doors and closed all their windows, even on hot summer days.

Kippernose shouted, 'Don't run away! I'll not hurt you! Please don't run away, I like

little people. I've only come to do my shopping. Please come out. I'll tell you a good story about a dragon and a mermaid.'

But it was no use. The town stayed silent and empty; the doors and windows stayed firmly closed. Poor Kippernose wanted so much to have someone to talk to. He felt so lonely that he often sat down in the town square and cried his heart out. You would think someone would take pity on him, but no one ever did. He simply couldn't understand it. He even tried going to another town, far across the mountains, but just the same thing happened.

'Has all the world gone mad?' said Kippernose to himself, and took his solitary way home.

The truth was that the people were not afraid of Kippernose, and they had not gone mad, either. The truth *was* . . . that Kippernose had not had a single bath in a hundred years, or more! The poor fellow carried such a stink wherever he went that everyone with a nose on his face ran for cover at

the first whiff. Oh, how that giant reeked! Pooh, you could smell him a mile away, and worst of all on hot days. People buried their noses in flowers and lavender-bags, but still the stench crept in. The wives cried shame and shame upon him, and swore that his stink turned their milk sour, and their butter rancid. What made matters worse, he never washed his hair or his whiskers, either. Smelly whiskers bristled all over his chin, and little creatures crept amongst them. His greasy hair fell down his back. He never used a comb. He never brushed his teeth. *And*, quite often, he went to bed with his boots on.

When he was a boy, Kippernose was always clean and smart, his mother saw to that. Long long ago, his good mother had gone off to live in far Cathay, and he had forgotten all she had told him about keeping clean and tidy, and changing his socks once a week. It was a lucky thing when his socks wore out, because that was the only time he would change them. He had no notion of the sight and smell he was. He never looked in a mirror. His smell had grown up with him, and he didn't notice it at all. His mind was deep among tales of dragons and wizards, for people in stories were his only friends. If only someone could have told him about his smell, in a nice way, all would have been well. The people grumbled enough amongst themselves. Mrs Dobson, of Ivy Cottage, was one of them. Friday was market day, and ironing day too, and every Friday night she would bang her iron angrily, and say to quiet Mr Dobson by the fireside, 'That giant's a scandal. It's every market day we have the sickening stench of him, and the whole pantry turned sour and rotten, too. Can't you men do something about it? You sit there and warm your toes, and nod off to sleep, while the world's going to ruin . . . '

'But, Bessie, my dear,' mild Mr Dobson answered, 'what can we do? You cannot expect anyone to go up to an enormous giant and say, "I say, old chap, you smell most dreadfully" – now can you? Besides, no one could get near enough to him: the smell would drive them away.'

'You could send him a letter,' said Mrs Dobson.

5

'But he cannot read. He never went to school. Even as a boy, Kippernose was too big to get through the school door, my old grandfather used to say.'

'Well, the government should do something about it,' said Mrs Dobson, banging on. 'If that Queen of ours came out of her palace and took a sniff of our Kippernose, *she'd* do something quickly enough, I'll bet.'

But it was not the Queen, or the government, or Mr Dobson, who solved the problem in the end. It was a creature so small that no one could see it.

One Friday in the middle of winter, a cold day of ice and fog, Kippernose went to town to do his shopping as usual. He felt so unhappy that he didn't even bother to call out and ask the people to stay to talk to him. He just walked gloomily into the market-place.

'It's no good,' he said to himself, 'they'll never be friends with me. They don't seem to think a giant has feelings like anyone else, I might just as well be . . . '

'Hoi! Look where you're going!' an angry

voice shouted up from the foggy street. 'Oh, I say, oh, help!' Then there was a great crash, and there were apples rolling everywhere. Then a babble of voices gathered round Kippernose.

'The clumsy great oaf – look, he's knocked Jim Surtees's apple-cart over. Did you ever see such a mess? Tramping about, not looking where he's going, with his head in the sky.'

Amongst all this angry noise stood Kippernose, with an enormous smile spreading across his big face. The smile grew to a grin.

'*They're not running away*. They're *not running away*,' said Kippernose, in a joyous whisper. Then he bent down, right down, and got down on his knees to bring his face near to the people.

'Why aren't you running away from me?' he said, softly, so as not to frighten them. 'Why aren't you running away as you always do? Please tell me, I beg of you.'

Jim Surtees was so angry that he had no fear of Kippernose, and he climbed upon his overturned apple-cart, and shouted up at him, 'Why, you great fool, it's because we cannot *smell* you.'

'Smell?' said Kippernose, puzzled.

'Yes; smell, stink, pong, stench; call it what you like,' said Jim.

'But I don't smell,' said Kippernose.

'Oh, yes you do!' all the people shouted together.

'You stink,' shouted Jim. 'You stink to the very heavens. That's why everyone runs away from you. It's too much for us – we just *have* to run away.'

'Why can't you smell me today?' said Kippernose.

'Because we've all caught a cold in the head for the first time in our lives, and our noses are stuffed up and runny, and we cannot smell anything, that's why,' said Jim. 'Some merchant came from England, selling ribbons, and gave us his germs as well. So we cannot smell you today, but next week we'll be better, and then see how we'll run.'

'But what can I do?' said Kippernose, looking so sad that even Jim felt sorry for him. 'I'm so lonely, with no one to talk to.'

'Well, you could take a bath,' said Jim.

'And you could wash your whiskers,' said Mrs Dobson. '. . . And your hair,' she added.

'*And* you could wash your clothes,' said Mr Dobson.

'*And* change your socks,' said Mrs Fox, eyeing his feet.

Distant memories stirred in Kippernose's head. 'Yes. Oh . . . yes. Mother did say something about all that, once, long ago; but I didn't take much notice. Do I really smell as bad as all that? Do I really?'

'Oh yes, you certainly do,' said Mrs Dobson. 'You smell a good deal worse than you can imagine. You turned my cheese green last week, *and* made Mrs Hill's baby cry for two hours without stopping when she left a window open by mistake. Oh, yes, you smell badly, Kippernose, as badly as anything could smell in this world.'

'If I do all you say, if I get all neat and clean, will you stop running away and be friends?' said Kippernose.

'Of course we will,' said Jim Surtees. 'We have nothing against giants. They can be useful if only they'll look where they're putting their feet, and they do say the giants were the best story-tellers in the old days.'

'Just you wait and see,' shouted Kippernose. As soon as he had filled his shopping basket, he walked purposefully off towards the hills. In his basket were one hundred and twenty bars of soap, and fifty bottles of bubble-bath!

That night Kippernose was busy as never before. Fires roared, and hot water gurgled in all the pipes of his house. There was such a steaming, and a splashing, and a gasping, and a bubbling, and a lathering, and a singing, and a laughing, as had not been heard in Kippernose's house for a hundred years. A smell of soap and bubble-bath drifted out upon the air, and even as far away as the town, people caught a whiff of it.

'What's that lovely smell?' said Mrs Dobson to her husband. 'There's a beautifully clean and scented smell that makes me think of a summer garden, even though it is the middle of winter.'

Then there was a bonfire of dirty old clothes in a field near Kippernose's farm, and a snip-snipping of hair and whiskers. Then there was a great rummaging in drawers and cupboards, and a shaking and airing of fresh clothes. The whole of that week, Kippernose was busy, so busy that he almost forgot to sleep and eat.

When Friday came round again, the people of the town saw an astonishing sight. Dressed in a neat Sunday suit, clean and clipped, shining in the wintry sun, and smelling of soap and sweet lavender, Kippernose strode towards them. He was a new Kippernose. The people crowded round him, and Jim Surtees shouted, 'Is it really you, Kippernose?'

'It certainly is,' said Kippernose, beaming joyously.

'Then you're welcome amongst us,' said Jim. 'You smell as sweetly as a flower, indeed you do, and I never thought you'd do it. Three cheers for good old Kippernose! Hip. Hip.'

And the crowd cheered,

'Hooray! Hooray! Hooray!'

Kippernose was never short of friends after that. He was so good and kind that all the people loved him, and he became the

11

happiest giant in all the world.

Ever afterwards, if any children would not go in the bath, or wash, or brush their teeth, or have their hair cut . . . then their mothers would tell them the story of Giant Kippernose.

This story is by John Cunliffe

Charlie Works a Miracle

Bonnie, the spaniel who lived with the Jacksons in the big bungalow down the road, had a litter of puppies, and Charlie wanted one. There were five in the litter and a rumour was going round the village that the pups would be sold for seventy-five pounds each when they were old enough to leave their mother.

'Seventy-five pounds!' exclaimed Mr Robinson when Charlie brought the subject up at breakfast. 'Well, all I can say is that some people have too much money to throw around.'

'Could we have a dog if it didn't cost too much?' asked Charlie.

Mr Robinson looked across the table.

'You'd better ask your mother,' he said. 'She'll be the one who'll have to clear up its messes.'

'I shouldn't mind,' said Mrs Robinson, 'and the messes don't last long, only until it's house-trained. Perhaps we could get one from the Dogs' Home.'

Charlie had nothing against dogs from the Dogs' Home, but he had set his heart on one of Bonnie's puppies. Then he heard that one of them had turned out to be much smaller than the others and would be sold for less than her brothers and sisters.

'I wonder how much it'll be,' said Charlie to Robert.

'Let's go and ask,' said Robert.

'Go and ask?' said Charlie in alarm. 'But I don't know the Jacksons. I've never been there in my life. They're very posh and horribly rich.'

'Well, you want the puppy, don't you?' said Tim, who was with them. 'I dare you.'

'All right,' said Charlie.

'You'd better go with him to see that he does it,' Tim said to Robert.

They went on Saturday afternoon. There

14

was nobody about, and their shoes scrunched noisily on the gravel as they walked up the drive, skirted a big ornamental pond filled with huge golden fish, and climbed the three shallow steps that led to the front door.

'You ring,' said Robert.

Charlie rang and Mrs Jackson herself opened the front door. Charlie had half-expected a maid or a butler.

'Hello,' she said. 'Is it Bob a Job week?'

'No,' said Charlie. 'We've come to see about the puppies.'

'Could we see them, please?' asked Robert.

'Of course,' said Mrs Jackson easily. 'Come in.'

She led them through the house, into an enormous kitchen fitted with every kind of gadget you could imagine, and then into another room where Bonnie was lying in a big wooden box with her puppies. She rose to greet her visitors, scattering puppies in all directions. She was black and white, and as far as Charlie could make out, two of her puppies were black all over and two were grey and white with black ears. There was no sign of the fifth until a tiny white head popped up between the broad backs of two of its brothers. It looked at Charlie out of a pair of bright blue eyes and began to wriggle and squirm its way out. It seemed to be all white except for a pair of black ears and a black smudge over one eye.

'Oh, please can I hold it?' asked Charlie.

'Of course,' said Mrs Jackson, and she pulled the puppy out of the litter and plumped it down into Charlie's outstretched arms. The puppy put out a tiny pink tongue and licked Charlie's forehead as he bent his face down to it. It felt soft and warm and fitted into his hands like a silky ball. Then Mr Jackson came in.

'Ha. Visitors,' he said.

'We've come to see the puppies,' said Charlie, who felt he ought to say something.

'Are your hands clean, boys?' asked Mr Jackson. 'Can't be too careful, you know. These are valuable pups. Can't afford to take risks.'

'I washed my hands before I came out,' said Charlie, glad for the first time in his life that his mother had won the hand-washing battle they had every day in his house. 'Have they all got homes?'

'All but the one you're holding,' said Mr Jackson.

'How much would this puppy cost?' asked Charlie, and in his anxiety, his hands tightened on the dog, which let out a little squeal.

'Don't squeeze her, dear,' said Mrs Jackson, taking the puppy and putting it back in the box, where Bonnie started to lick it.

'Sixty pounds,' said Mr Jackson, 'and that's cheap. The others are going for seventy-five. But she's a good little bitch. Make somebody a fine pet.'

Charlie and Robert had nothing to say except to thank Mrs Jackson for letting them see the puppies as she took them to the front door.

'He must be joking,' said Robert when they were in the road once more.

'He wasn't,' said Charlie. 'Old skinflint. Filthy money bags. But I do want that puppy. I'm going to pray for a miracle.'

17

'They only happen in the Bible,' said
Robert.

'They don't. My dad said it was a miracle
when the Bank Manager let him have a loan
to start his Driving School business.'

'Go on,' said Robert scornfully. 'A
miracle's something like the loaves and
the fishes.'

Weeks passed. The puppies grew up,

and one by one went to live with people who could afford seventy-five pounds. Charlie wondered whether the Jacksons had managed to sell the smallest one. He stopped at their gate one evening when Mr Jackson was cleaning out his fishpond.

'Have you sold the tiny puppy yet?' asked Charlie.

'Not yet,' said Mr Jackson. 'She's called Smudge, by the way – black smudge over her eye, you know.'

'I could give her a home if you want to get rid of her,' said Charlie. 'If you drop the price a bit – quite a bit.'

19

'Come in if you want to talk business,' said Mr. Jackson. 'And I can clean out the pond while we're talking.'

Charlie went in and stood with Mr Jackson beside the pool. The fish really were enormous, as big as the trout in the reservoir.

'Aren't the goldfish huge?' he said.

'They're carp,' said Mr Jackson firmly. 'And this little collection is worth something, I can tell you. Now, did you say your family wanted to buy Smudge?'

'How much would she cost?' asked Charlie.

Mr Jackson considered. 'Hm . . . last time I saw you I said sixty, didn't I? Well, I'll do you a favour, call it fifty-five.'

'Pounds?' said Charlie, to whom fifty-five pence was a fortune.

'Pounds,' said Mr Jackson.

'But she's very tiny,' said Charlie, 'and I thought perhaps as nobody seems to want her that you might sell her to me very cheaply. I'd take great care of her and look after her properly.'

'Look, laddie,' said Mr Jackson. 'Business

is business and don't you forget it. I only got where I am now by remembering that.'

'My dad hasn't got fifty-five pounds,' said Charlie.

'Then I'm afraid you'll have to give up the idea.'

'I told Robert only a miracle would make you change your mind,' said Charlie, who was so disappointed he didn't care whether he sounded rude or not.

'Who's Robert?'

'The boy who came with me to see the puppies. He said miracles only happen in the Bible.'

' 'Fraid they do,' agreed Mr Jackson cheerfully.

'Letting me have your puppy for free would be a miracle that's not in the Bible,' said Charlie.

'Yes,' said Mr Jackson, 'and if the water in my carp pond turned bright green, I suppose you'd call that a miracle, but that sort of thing doesn't happen.'

'I know,' said Charlie. He turned miserably away and made for the gate.

'Tell you what,' said Mr Jackson. Charlie

21

looked round. 'If my carp pond ever turns bright green, I'll give you the pup for free. How's that, eh? You start praying for a miracle, my boy.' Charlie left him laughing at his own joke. He didn't see anything to laugh at and was miserable for days afterwards whenever he thought of Smudge.

He cheered up a bit near the end of term, when Miss Clarke hired a coach to take the Lower Juniors on an outing. They visited a Nature Trail on the Mendips. They had a picnic first, and then they scrambled down into a little valley where a stream was bubbling through brambles and fern over a stony bed. They followed it until suddenly it disappeared and the stony gully ran on without any water in it.

'Where's the water gone?' asked Annie Thomas.

Miss Clarke explained how lots of streams in the hills around them did that. 'They run through underground limestone passages,' she said, 'and sometimes they come out above the ground for a little way lower down the hill and plunge again under the rock and come out in the valley.'

'Like the Underground in London,' said Tim, who had been there. 'We got on at Paddington and we went through a tunnel and stayed underneath the ground for ages, but when we got to South Kensington, where we were getting out, we were in the open air again.'

'That's right,' said Miss Clarke.

'Do the streams in Easting come through the ground like that?' asked Charlie.

'Most of them do,' said Miss Clarke.

'Gosh,' said Charlie. He took a matchbox out of his pocket (he always had a matchbox or two on him, they came in very useful) and put it into the stream. It bobbed gently along for a few centimetres and then got stuck against a stone. He lifted it off and sent it on its travels once more.

'Don't litter the countryside, Charlie,' said Miss Clarke. 'If you have anything to throw away, keep it for the rubbish box on the coach and we'll take it back to the school dustbin.'

Charlie didn't think it worth explaining that his matchbox was an experiment, that it was supposed to follow the stream through all its winding way underground until it came out one day in Easting. He picked it out of the water, dried it on his handkerchief and stuffed it back into his pocket.

He tried again when the others had all moved off and nobody was looking. This time he put the matchbox right where a stream disappeared into the ground. Nothing happened, the matchbox stuck there, because there was no real opening, no black tunnel to go through like there was on the London Underground. How did people know that these streams came out into Easting and all the other places? It couldn't be done by floating things down them. He picked up his matchbox and ran after the others.

After the outing, Charlie was very busy practising for the school Sports Day and he had little time to think about the Jackson puppy. Then one day Mrs Robinson picked him up from school with Lucinda and drove off without waiting to talk to the other mothers.

'You're in for it, you are,' she said to

Charlie. 'I don't know how you could do such a stupid thing.'

'Do what?' asked Charlie. 'I haven't done anything.'

'It's lucky your father was home early today,' said Mrs Robinson. 'I couldn't have coped with Mr Jackson on my own.'

She wouldn't say another word, and when they reached home, she hauled Charlie towards the sitting-room, where he could hear someone speaking in a loud angry voice.

'Well, here he is,' he heard his father say.

Mr Robinson was standing with his back to the fireplace, while Mr Jackson was pacing up and down the room. He turned on Charlie. 'What do you mean by it?' he demanded. 'How dare you? Because you and that friend of yours have visited my house, you needn't think you can . . . ' Words failed him.

Charlie stood stiff and still. He reached out and clutched his mother's hand. Mr Robinson saw Charlie's white face. 'I'll ask him about it,' he said. 'Sit down, Charlie. Let's all sit down.'

Mr Jackson threw himself on the sofa and muttered something about calling the police. Mr Robinson looked gravely at Charlie. 'Do you know anything about Mr Jackson's pond?' he asked.

'No, Dad,' said Charlie.

'Of course he does,' raved Mr Jackson.

'Please,' said Mr Robinson. He turned to Charlie. 'Mr Jackson thinks you have been fooling around with his pond. Now come on, what do you know about it?'

'Nothing,' said Charlie. 'I haven't been near his pond. Honest, Dad.'

'Then he put his friends up to it,' snapped Mr Jackson.

'Up to what?' asked Charlie. 'What's been going on, Dad?'

'Mr Jackson says you've done something to the colour of his pond.'

'What!' Charlie leaped up with sparkling eyes and looked at Mr Jackson. 'Is it green?' he asked.

'You'll pay for it,' said Mr Jackson. 'Pay for the water to be pumped out, pay for the fish too if they've been poisoned.'

'Charlie, just what have you been doing?' asked Mr Robinson wearily.

'Nothing,' said Charlie. 'It's a miracle.'

Mr Jackson made a choking noise and it was another quarter of an hour before the Robinsons pieced together the story of the puppy and the miracle from the bewildered Charlie and the raging Mr Jackson. The pond had been quite normal at eight o'clock that morning when Mr Jackson left for work, but by three o'clock in the afternoon it had turned bright green. Mrs Jackson had telephoned her husband at his office and he had come home early. Mr Robinson persuaded Mr Jackson to go home and promised to telephone him in the morning. When Robert came up to play with Charlie after tea, Mr Robinson questioned them both, but Robert had no more idea than Charlie how the water had changed colour.

In school next day, Charlie kept expecting to see a policeman walk in to arrest him. When school was over and he was still a free citizen, he went into Mr Ford's field below the garden to think things out and be away from Mr Jackson if he came round again. Robert and Tim came up and joined him beside the ditch.

'I wish old Jackson would drown in his

rotten pond,' said Robert.

'Are you sure you didn't do it by just thinking about it?' asked Tim. 'Perhaps you've got special powers. Kine -- something it's called. There was this film where a girl wanted to get her own back on everybody and she willed things to happen like a dance hall falling down on people at a disco and they all died horrible deaths like being electrocuted and having ceilings falling down on them.'

'Oh shut up,' said Charlie. 'I didn't do anything. I don't know how his beastly water turned green.'

'I say,' Robert's voice sounded very odd. 'Look, Charlie, you've done it again. The water in the ditch has turned green while we've been sitting here.' They scooped the water out in their hands, and it was definitely green.

'It's nothing to do with me,' said Charlie.

'Are you sure you aren't willing it?' asked Tim.

'No I'm not,' snapped Charlie. He felt frightened. 'I'm going home and you needn't come.' He scrambled through the hedge and ran up the garden path. He was going to shut himself in his bedroom and not come out until all the water round the place had settled down to its normal colour.

He arrived indoors to find the house full of people. He stood miserably in the doorway of the sitting-room and looked around. At least there weren't any policemen. Mr Jackson was there with Mrs Jackson, who was holding Smudge. His mother and father were there, and Lucinda, and three strangers, two young men in anoraks and an older man in a grey suit. Except for Lucinda, they were all drinking sherry. No one seemed to be annoyed any more, in fact they all looked very friendly.

Mrs Jackson smiled. 'Here he is,' she said, and turned to her husband, who came forward to stand in front of Charlie. He looked very embarrassed and didn't seem to know what to say. Suddenly, he took Smudge from his wife's arms and held her out to Charlie.

'She's yours,' he said. 'Can't go back on my word. Yours for free, like I said. But it was an odd sort of miracle. Sorry to have

29

doubted you, old chap. Wasn't anything to do with you, it was these Johnnies here.' He indicated the three strangers. 'Anyway, look after the pup. If you want any advice, ask us.'

Charlie sat down suddenly on the nearest chair, clutching Smudge. His legs seemed to have gone wrong. The puppy reached up and licked his face.

'But what's happened?' he asked. 'The water in the ditch is green as well.'

The man in the grey suit smiled. 'That's us, I'm afraid. The Water Board.' He explained that his assistants, the two young men in anoraks, had been putting dye into the streams at the top of the hill to trace the underground water courses and find out where each one came to the surface lower down. 'We're planning to build a small reservoir in Easting and it helps us to know where all the water comes from and goes to,' he said.

One of the young men said, 'We were using red and green dyes. They're quite harmless and we have been able to reassure Mr Jackson that his fish will be all right. Their pond is fed by an underground stream which comes up in his garden, so some of the dye landed up there.'

'It might have been red,' said the other young man. 'I was using the red dye, but it was Ted's green stuff that came into East-ing.'

'Of course it was,' said Charlie happily. 'It had to be green to work the miracle.'

This story is by Sylvia Woods

The Magician Who Kept a Pub

There was once a Magician who kept a pub. This pub stood in a market square in an English country town. It was called The Golden Pig and was famous throughout the land.

And why was it famous?

Wouldn't you expect it to be famous if it had a Magician for a landlord? A Magician who walked about all day with his coat open to show off a waistcoat that was sewn all over with diamonds and sapphires and emeralds? Why, that waistcoat was so dazzling that when the Magician stood outside his door enjoying the morning sunshine it flashed and sparkled with every twist and turn of him, filling the air with the wildness of gypsy fiddles.

...en there was the sign that hung above
... public bar door. That was a famous thing
in itself. A swinging pig in solid gold – deep
red-gold, picked out all over in fiery rubies,
so bright and flaming and daunting it was
when the sun shone strong upon it that it
throbbed and boomed like a great gong
with vibrations that set the striped awnings
over the market-stalls quivering until their
colours seemed to run together.

And there was the Magician's daughter
who was so beautiful it made you blink
to look at her. She had hair as fine as spun
moonlight that she brushed each morning
leaning from her window high above The
Golden Pig, and as she brushed the lively
strands fanned out across the brick-work
and when she shook them loose it was like
a waterfall – the rush and tinkle and splash
of it!

Imagine the splendid glitter and flash
and clash when the morning sun fell
booming upon that red-gold pig and flashed
and winked in the jewels of that twinkling
waistcoat and ran sunbeams among the

moonbeam tresses of the landlord's lovely daughter as she leaned brushing her rustling hair as it fell like a waterfall, cool in the sunlight. What a poetic sight! No wonder people came to stare!

On the other side of the square three brothers kept three market-stalls, which they set up every day and minded until evening came. Len, Les and Arnie they were called.

Len the eldest was the sharp one, the sly, keen brother. He sold fish, did Len. Every day he cried, 'Sprats and mackerel all a-fresh-o! Whelks, plaice and 'addocks still wet from the sea!

' 'Ere you are, lady, smell the salt if you don't believe me!' he'd say, sliding his crafty eyes.

The next brother, Les, was the artful one, the lazy dodger. He sold fruit and vegetables: 'Apples a pound pears! Nothing wrong with my stuff. Don't mind the specks, lady – good for the complexion.

'What about this, sir – a pair of cauliflowers for the price of two? Thank you very much. Your change, guv.' That was Les.

That leaves Arnie. He was the youngest and the softest: the dreamer.

Arnie sold things made of wood. Chairs and tables, cupboards and butter-tubs – things he had made himself. Arnie never shouted his wares. He was the quiet brother, the one who sat and waited till his customers came, and was quite disappointed when they did as he was so attached to the things he had made.

And, of course, all three of them wanted to marry the pub-keeper's daughter – the Magician's child!

Fishmonger Len looked across each day and said, 'Cor – that weskit. It throws me. What a sparkler. Just think – every now and then he could pick off a bit of trimming and sell it for a little fortune. Oh, wouldn't I like to be that old geezer's son-in-law and come in for that weskit one day!'

Les said, 'When I think of that golden porker over there – solid gold and all those rubies – worth a bomb. Brother! I'd like to marry the Magician's daughter for the chance of one day being able to run my fingers through a heap of those red flashers.'

But Arnie, our hero, he would stand staring; seeing only the Magician's lovely daughter twirling and pinning and plaiting her moonlight tresses, and, sighing to himself, would wonder what it would be like to pull out those hair-pins and let the soft hair flow forth again. 'Oh how beautiful she is,' he said.

At last Len, the first brother, took his courage in his hands and went across the market square and spoke to the Magician as he stood outside his pub looking up and down the street.

'You know me, guv,' said Len, in a sly and wheedling voice, his eyes fixed greedily on that jewelled waistcoat, 'I'm Scaly Len the fishmonger from over the square. Many a fat kipper I've sent over for your breakfast and many a choice winkle I've boiled for your landlordship's tea.

'You have only got to look across the road to see that I do good business. It must be plain to you that I can support a missus. And, between you and me, you'll never lack a shrimp for your tea as long as I can provide it – so how about considering me for a son-in-law?'

And all the time he spoke his gaze was on the waistcoat, and every word he spoke he said to it.

The Magician looked hard at Len for a moment, then he said, 'Well, that's easier said than done. For why? Well, I can't give my gal away to someone for nothing. Oh no!

'No. I've got a fancy. Just as you've got a fancy say – for my weskit – or my daughter, I've got a fancy to eat one of the rare silver eggs from the wishing-bird's nest for breakfast on my daughter's wedding day.

'If you could get me one of those, you can have my girl for your wife and everything else – I reckon I'd retire after eating a breakfast like that.' And he rolled his wicked eyes and grinned like the devil.

But Len whose own eyes were dazzled by the white and green and blue dance of that restless waistcoat did not notice the grin. He licked his lips in anticipation and said, 'It's as good as done, guv. Just tell me where I can find that silver egg in the wishing-bird's nest and it's yours for the boiling!'

The Magician grinned again, 'Do you know that high sky-scraping block of flats right at the edge of the town?'

Len said, 'You mean that very high one – the one that's so high its roof is lost in the clouds?'

'The highest in the world. That's right!' said the Magician pub-keeper. 'Well now, right up on the top there, above the cloud-line – up among the TV aerials, the wishing-bird has made her nest. And on it she sits, day and night, trying to hatch out her silver eggs.

'It wouldn't be difficult to slip your hand into her nest and take one of them – if she's so stupid as to think she can hatch out silver eggs, she'd be too stupid to notice a sly one like you.'

And he chuckled as he spoke and Len joined him with a snigger. 'It sounds easy as pie,' he said. 'Yes, I'll have a go.'

To himself he thought, 'What a fool this old Magician is – not to have tried to get one himself. And what a fool-and-a-half he is to talk of eating a silver egg that can't be hatched out!'

But, as he turned to go, the Magician who knew every single thought that had passed through his head, and was grinning like a demon, said softly, 'Wait wait, my dear young man! Surely you didn't think there'd be no conditions? Why, in situations like this there are always conditions!'

Len stopped and looked straight at the Magician, who met his gaze with a smile as mild as milk.

'There are lifts in that building of course – lifts from the cellars below the basement right to the roof above. But the condition is: THAT YOU DON'T USE THEM. The condition is that you use the stairs that climb alongside the lifts. You have to mount by those stairs. No lifts mind – and the other condition is that you keep a civil tongue in your head.'

As he spoke the waistcoat glowed like fairy-lamps to match the gentleness of his voice.

'Use the stairs – civil tongue. Right!' replied Len. 'Any more? No? Then I'm off.' And off he ran, so eager to possess the Magician's waistcoat he didn't hear the rest of the Magician's words: ' —and no cheating when there is magic about. Cheating can be very, very dangerous.'

By then Len had reached the place where his little fish-van was parked behind the town hall. With a roar and a rush he was off. And in less than twelve minutes – so favourable were the traffic lights – green all the way – he arrived at the tall, tall building – the high block of flats. Looking up and up, he saw the white clouds clinging about the rooftop and concealing the highest storeys and below them rows of windows small as pin-pricks, twinkling in the sunshine so far up they were.

'Well, this is IT,' said Len the sharp brother, slamming his van door and locking it.

There was no one and nothing inside the great echoing entrance hall. Only a long row of lift-doors like gilded gates. As Len stepped towards them one glided open. But Len was too sharp for that.

'No no! Naughty, naughty,' he said, 'I'm for the staircase – like the gentleman said.' And passing the lifts he found the beginning of a stone staircase and began to climb, up and up to a landing and up and up again.

He had gone up three flights when he heard a strange sound – a scrubbing noise, and there, kneeling on the second step of the next flight, he found an old, old woman, with a great bucket of soapy water beside her, scrubbing away.

'Mind my step. Mind my step,' the old woman cried. 'Don't walk on it, it's wet!'

'All right, Ma,' said sharp Len, keeping a civil tongue in his head, 'keep your wig on. I'll hop over it.'

And that's what he did, while the old woman muttered to herself. And on he went, on and on and up and up and then—

'No, not her again,' said Len. But there she was, the same old woman, scrubbing away.

'Mind out, don't tread on my step. It's clean,' she said, and Len, whose legs were a bit tired, held on to the hand-rail and pulled himself over it, and went up rather slowly until, there on the next landing he met her again, scrubbing away at a step. This landing

42

was wide and to reach the next flight he had
to pass an open lift-door.

'Oh no, oh no,' said Len to himself, 'it's
climbing for me,' and though his calves were
killing him and his ankles were now numb,
he managed to heave himself over the old
woman's step.

'She must get ahead of me by travelling
on the lift,' he thought.

And this went on until he got to the
seventy-fifth floor where again there was an
open lift. This time the old woman could be
heard scrubbing a step high up on the next
flight.

'I've had enough of this,' Len said. 'My
knees are weak as paper and that old girl is
enough to tempt anyone to be rude. If it's
a civil tongue I've got to have, there's only
one thing for it – I'll take the lift the rest of
the way. After all, who's to tell on me?'

And saying this, he crept into the
open door of the nearest lift, pressed
the button that said, 'Roof only' and . . .
dropped. Down, down in the lift, faster than
light, faster than sound, down to the cellars
below the basement, and rolled out, as the

lift-doors opened – in the shape of a small, black pebble!

And there he stayed.

Now you might imagine that his brother Les would have been worried when he didn't return. But he wasn't. He was very pleased, he saw it paving the way for himself. It was Arnie who went to the police, and, as they could find nothing out, it was he who took over Len's fish-stall and ran it along with his own until such time as his sharp brother could be found.

It wasn't long before Les was trying his luck with the Magician. With his head full of the golden pig and his ears dinning with the richness of red-gold and rubies he crossed the square and entered the saloon bar, where the landlord was busily drawing foaming pints for his regular customers.

These regulars were a devilish looking crowd, and when they saw Les they began to snicker among themselves, but he did not notice them – especially as the landlord was very civil to him when Les said that he'd come to ask for his daughter's hand.

The Magician said the same thing to

him that he had to his brother.

And Les, wild with excitement, stuttered and said, 'Oh yes, your pig-ship, I mean lordship, my highly honoured publican, sir. I do understand. No, your ruby-ship, I won't even look at a lift – feet all the time. Civil tongue, sir. Of course, sir. No cheating! What a hurtful suggestion,' and gave an artful, ingratiating smile, and left the bar, bowing to right and left as if acknowledging his dearest friends, while the strange regulars shook with mirth.

'He would marry my golden pig, would he? We'll see about that,' said the Magician as the door closed behind him.

And soon enough, Les arrived in his van at the block of skyscraper flats, and soon, like Len before him, he was mounting the stairs. Up he went. Not as fast as Len had done. Steadily, using his artful wits to conserve his strength, but even so, by the time he had mounted some twenty flights he was certainly tired. That was when he met the old woman scrubbing as before. 'Look out,' she called, 'mind my step. Don't tread on my step, I've just cleaned it.'

He wasn't very pleased, but he remembered about a civil tongue, so he just said he was sorry and stepped carefully over the wet step.

She was on the next flight, then the next and the one after that. She was still there when he reached the eighty-second flight. By now he was huffing and puffing as much as his brother Len had been; now his calves were weak as paper and his ankles bent inwards from the strain.

And there was the horrible old woman, scrubbing and complaining. 'Mind out, mind out,' she yelled. 'Don't tread on my step. What do you want to come up this way for? What do you think the lifts are for?'

At last Les showed his temper – he'd lost it long ago. 'Trying to tempt me to use the lift, eh?' he snarled. 'To blazes with your horrible bucket.'

And in spite of his tiredness, he raised his foot, and aimed a strong kick that sent the old woman's bucket bumping away down the steps, rolling across the landings, and clattering down the next flight, and the next and the next . . . and after the bucket, down, down and down bounced a round black stone, falling from step to step along landings and down again till it descended to the cellars below the basement where it rolled and came to a stop beside a black stone that was already lying there.

Yes, Les was now a black pebble like his brother Len, and there they lay, side by side, on the floor of the lowest cellar of the tall block of flats.

So poor Arnie was left all alone to mind the three market-stalls as best he could. Across the square the golden pig still glowed with rubies, the Magician's waistcoat still flashed and sparkled, and his lovely daughter still brushed her moonlight hair.

The police from five counties began chasing clues – they had a theory that Len and Les had been members of a smuggling gang. They had carefully searched the abandoned vans and found nothing but cods' heads and fish-scales in the one and old potatoes and withered leeks in the other; but they were far from satisfied.

Now Arnie was very busy indeed. He

felt he must keep his brothers' businesses going as well as his own so, as his only day off was Sunday, he had to leave it until then before he in his turn tried his hand at wooing the Magician's daughter.

But unlike Len and Les, Arnie did not go to the Magician. After all, it wasn't him he wanted to marry. No, he waited about the empty market square for an hour or so while he plucked up courage, and then he crossed the road, walked past the pub's swinging doors, and went in round the back through the gates the brewers' lorries used.

Here in the yard, he found the landlord's daughter, busily stacking dirty glasses in a vast washing-up machine. He was surprised to see how short she was – even with her heaped mass of hair – and glad to see how sweet she was – even sweeter than he'd imagined her to be when he'd fallen in love.

Awkwardly, because he was so overcome with emotion, he poured out his proposal.

'If you will marry me,' he said, 'I'll take you away from all this. We will live in the little cottage in the woods that my godmother left me – I'll cut wood and make chairs and tables, beds and cupboards for it. And a strong oak cradle to rock our babies in.

'And you,' he said sentimentally, 'will sit all day on the doorstep brushing your moonbeam hair.'

'I,' said the landlord's daughter practically, 'will be on the telephone or dictating letters to my secretary. I will be selling all the lovely furniture that you will go on making after we are married.'

She smiled at him, and he saw that her eyes were like sapphires, and her lips were like rubies. 'I fell in love with you a long time ago,' she said. 'I used to watch you when I was brushing my hair. How you stared! That's why I took so long doing it in the morning – I brushed it for you.

'I know you are a dreamy impractical fellow,' she said lovingly, 'or you'd never have let your brothers get in first. But that suits me very well, for I have a managing, business head on me.'

So they embraced, there in the yard before the washing-up machine full of glasses and tankards, and it was there the Magician found them.

The Magician stood regarding them for a moment and then he gave a loud cough, so that they sprang apart and looked sheepish. His daughter, however, quickly recovered her wits.

'You might as well know it, Dad,' she said, 'Arnie and I are engaged to be married.'

The Magician gave a sour smile. 'He hasn't asked me for my permission,' he said. 'Why didn't you?' he said to Arnie. 'Why didn't you speak to me first?'

Arnie turned cherry-red, but he held his ground, polite to his future father-in-law he intended to be, but he wasn't going to be brow-beaten. 'I wasn't really interested in what you thought, sir,' he said. 'It's what your daughter thought that mattered. After all, if she hadn't cared for me you couldn't have made her marry me against her will. Not in this day and age, anyway.'

The Magician's daughter laughed, and squeezed his arm. 'Well said,' she told him.

'No, Dad,' she said to her father. 'You know you couldn't have forced me. Just what would you have done if one of

Arnie's brothers had been successful? I wouldn't have considered either of them for a minute. You'd have had to part with your waistcoat or your pub-sign in lieu of me, I'm thinking.'

'It was hardly likely either of them would have succeeded anyway,' the Magician said, ' – neither of them had the character for success. I doubt very much if this one could manage to get the silver egg either – no one has ever beaten me at my own game, and I've a trick or two up my sleeve, believe me.'

'The lengths you'll go to keep that nasty old sign and that flashy old waistcoat,' said his daughter scornfully.

'But I don't want either of them,' said Arnie mildly. 'All I ever wanted was your beautiful daughter. And it looks as if I've got her, anyway.'

The Magician thought for a moment, and then he smiled, and then he laughed. Out from the saloon bar swarmed the Magician's regulars – and they were laughing too.

Suddenly the Sunday bells began to chime from the church steeple, sending a whole

flock of white pigeons up into the air from
the belfry tower.

Suddenly the whole square was filled
with little girls in white pinafores trotting
off to Sunday School, and sweet old ladies
and gentlemen in their Sunday best hobbling
to church.

'So it's no silver egg, eh?' asked the
Magician.

For answer his daughter put two fingers
to her ruby lips and whistled shrill as any
street-boy.

At once the air was filled with the beating
sound of great wings, the daylight darkened
as something passed between the earth and

the sun. There was a clicking of claws and
a scraping of quills, and suddenly the yard
was filled with the stuffy dusty feathers of a
vast and stupid-looking bird – a bird that was
trying to balance itself upon the washing-up
machine.

'The wishing-bird,' said the Magician's
daughter proudly. 'No need to climb if you

know the correct signal.

'Lay an egg for us,' she said commandingly, and the stupid creature did just that – laid a fine silver egg that rolled into the washing–up machine and lay among the wet glasses.

'And something else?' said the Magician's daughter. The bird opened its beak, and there on its tongue lay two black pebbles.

'Your brothers, I think,' she said to Arnie.

Then, to her father, 'Come on now, Dad, change them back and don't mess about.'

Looking thoroughly abashed in front of his regulars, whose admiring glances were fixed on his resolute child, the Magician obliged by making a few magic passes and muttering a few strange words. And there, dishevelled from their adventure, and damp from having travelled in the bird's mouth, stood Len and Les! Both, it is to be hoped, wiser and better men.

Next day they returned to their stalls in the market, and in spite of the suspicions of the police they conducted themselves so well that in time they became prosperous from their own industry. Whilst Len never could afford a jewelled waistcoat, he managed to buy himself a real dazzler of a watch and chain with charms and dangleums of gold encrusted with jewels. Les eventually moved into a very big greengrocer's shop, with a sign overhead of a golden pineapple. It was only gold-leaf to be sure, but he made up for it by having a fat little wife upon whom he bestowed a real ruby necklace and a ruby ring.

And Arnie and the Magician's daughter? They went to live in the little house in the woods as Arnie had hoped. Arnie makes furniture from the trees in the wood, and the Magician's daughter manages the sales. They are both very happy, and every night Arnie sits entranced as he watches her brush her moonlight hair.

Len and Les and the Magician are now great friends – they spend many hours in the saloon bar talking over old times, or standing treat to the regulars.

As for the stupid wishing-bird she still sits on top of the high tower-block laying her silver eggs. You might try getting one for yourself some time – that is, if you can manage such a climb and can keep your patience with that old woman.

This story is by Dorothy Edwards

Campers

Mummy was changing Christopher's nappy when the front doorbell rang.

'Jeremy James, would you please see who it is!' called Mummy from upstairs, and Jeremy James stood on tip-toe to open the front door. Standing on the step were Mrs Smyth-Fortescue from next door, and her son Timothy, who was a year older than Jeremy James and knew all about everything.

'Hello, Jeremy,' said Mrs Smyth-Fortescue, who never called him Jeremy *James*. 'Is your mummy in?'

'Yes, Mrs Smyth-Forciture,' said Jeremy James, who never said Smyth-*Fortescue*, 'but Christopher's just done a pong.'

'Ah, she's changing him, is she?' asked

Mrs Smyth-Fortescue.

'No,' said Jeremy James, 'I think she's going to keep him.'

Mummy came down the stairs. 'Hello, Mrs Smyth-Fortescue,' she said. 'Won't you come in?'

'No, we can't stop,' said Mrs Smyth-Fortescue. 'We just popped round to see if Jeremy would like to spend the night in Timothy's new tent. We bought it yesterday – frightfully expensive, but his old one was falling to bits, and he did so want this new one. It's the best on the market.'

'I'm sure he'd like to,' said Mummy.

'Jeremy's such good company for Timothy,' said Mrs Smyth-Fortescue. 'And they get on so nicely together.'

Timothy looked at Jeremy James and held his nose, and Jeremy James poked out his tongue at Timothy.

'Would you like that, Jeremy James?' asked Mummy.

'Ugh . . . hmmph . . . well . . . ' said Jeremy James.

'Timothy doesn't want to sleep there on his own,' said Mrs Smyth-Fortescue, 'and I'm . . . well, ha ha . . . a little past such things, you know. My husband would keep Timothy company, but he's away on business. In America this time. Such a bore.'

'You'd love to sleep in Timothy's tent, wouldn't you, Jeremy James?' asked Mummy.

'Hmmph . . . well . . . ugh . . . ' said Jeremy James.

'Oh good, I'm so glad,' said Mrs Smyth-Fortescue. 'Then that's settled. The tent's already up in the back garden, and I'll cook them a lovely barbecue supper. Do you like sausages, Jeremy?'

'Well, yes,' said Jeremy James.

'And baked beans and chips?'

Jeremy James did like baked beans and chips, and he liked sausages, and he liked the idea of sleeping in a tent. It was just a pity that Timothy would have to be there as well.

'Good,' said Mrs Smyth-Fortescue. 'We'll see you later, Jeremy.'

'Yes, Mrs Smyth-Torcyfue,' said Jeremy James.

'Big pong,' said Timothy.

'And so are you,' said Jeremy James.

The new tent was a beauty. It was high enough for the boys to stand in, and apart from the two airbeds, one on either side of the central pole, there was even room for a little table and two little chairs. And here they sat as Mrs Smyth-Fortescue served them with sausages, baked beans and chips, Coca-Cola and ice-cream. She left them gobbling like a couple of starved turkeys, and for minutes on end there was no sound but contented munching, slurping and burping.

When eventually they had finished, Jeremy James put his dessert plate on his dinner plate, and his glass on his dessert plate, and sat back feeling rather pleased with life.

'You've never been camping before!' said Timothy.

Jeremy James felt slightly less pleased with life. 'Hmmph!' he said.

'Real campers don't put their dishes like that,' said Timothy. 'Anybody who knows anything about camping knows you don't put dishes like that!'

'Well, how do you put dishes, then?' asked Jeremy James.

'You leave them – like this,' said Timothy, indicating his own dishes spread out over the table.

'My mummy says you should put your dishes like this!' said Jeremy James, indicating his neat little pile.

'Then your mummy doesn't know anything about camping either,' said Timothy.

Just then Mrs Smyth-Fortescue arrived to collect the dirty dishes. 'Oh, what a good boy, Jeremy,' she said. 'Piling up your dishes so nicely.'

'My mother's never been camping either,' said Timothy, when Mrs Smyth-Fortescue had gone. 'It's only men who know about camping.'

'You're not a man,' said Jeremy James.

'I will be soon,' said Timothy. 'Much sooner than you.'

'Well, if you're such a man,' said Jeremy James, 'why were you scared to sleep in the tent on your own?'

'Scared?' said Timothy. 'SCARED??? Me??? I'll show you who's scared!'

Whereupon he hurled himself at Jeremy James, and as he was much bigger and heavier, it was not long before he was sitting on Jeremy James's chest, with his knees pinning Jeremy James's arms to the ground.

'Now who's scared?' asked Timothy, scowling down.

'Just because you're bigger than me,' said Jeremy James, 'it doesn't prove you're not . . . ouch!'

Timothy had leaned forward, squashing

Jeremy James's head with his chest.

'Having a nice game, dears?' came the voice of Mrs Smyth-Fortescue. 'You'd better go to the bathroom now, before it gets really dark. Timothy, get off Jeremy.'

'Can't,' said Timothy.

'Come along, Jeremy,' said Mrs Smyth-Fortescue. 'Let Timothy get off now.'

Eventually Mrs Smyth-Fortescue made Jeremy James let go of Timothy's knees with his arms, and release Timothy's bottom from his chest, and the two boys went to the house to wash their hands and faces, and clean their teeth. But Timothy didn't wash and didn't clean his teeth, because he said campers never did.

By the time they were tucked up in bed, the night was as black as Timothy's knees. Mrs Smyth-Fortescue had left them a torch which Timothy said only he should have, because he was the one that knew about camping. He shone it a few times in Jeremy James's eyes, but then he began to shine it round the tent, and the beam came to rest on the door-flap. 'Do you think a lion could get through the door?' he asked.

63

'I expect so,' said Jeremy James. 'Your mother got in, didn't she?'

'My mother's not a lion,' said Timothy.

'She's the same size as a lion,' said Jeremy James. 'But a bit fatter.'

There was a moment's silence. The torch continued to shine on the flap.

'A ghost could get in, too,' said Timothy.

'Ghosts can get in anywhere,' said Jeremy James. 'Ghosts can even get into your bedroom. And so can spiders.'

'Ugh!' said Timothy.

There was a noise outside the tent – a padding noise.

'What's that?' came Timothy's terrified whisper.

'I don't know,' whispered Jeremy James. 'Put the light out, so it won't know we're here!'

Timothy switched off the torch. There was more padding, then a snuffle-whiffle-snort, then silence. Then more silence.

'Has it gone?' whispered Timothy.

'Don't know,' whispered Jeremy James.

More silence. No more padding. No more snuffles. WHOO WHOO!

'W . . . w . . . wa . . . what's that?'
Timothy's voice came out in a hoarse
wobble.

'That's an owl,' said Jeremy James. 'No
need to be scared of an owl!'

WHOO WHOO! WHOO WHOO!

'S . . . sou . . . sounds like a g . . .
gug . . . ghost to me,' said Timothy.

'Ghosts say BOO, not WHOO,' said
Jeremy James.

'S . . . s . . . some gug . . . gug . . .

ghosts s . . . say WHOO!' said Timothy.

But boo-saying and whoo-saying ghosts didn't really matter any more to Jeremy James. The weight of the sausages, beans and chips had begun to shift from his tummy to his eyes, and when his eyes closed, his ears closed, too. Only his imagination stayed awake, supplying him with dreams of Mrs Smyth-Fortescue roaring on all fours, and of himself being pinned to the ground by a string of sausages.

When Jeremy James woke up the next morning, he was surrounded by a glow of orange and green, which he soon realized was the sun shining into the tent and on to the grass. The other thing he soon realized was that Timothy's bed and sleeping bag were still there, and Timothy's clothes were still there, but Timothy himself was most definitely not there.

Perhaps, thought Jeremy James with a little smile, a lion had gobbled Timothy up in the night. Or a ghost might have taken him off to the Land of Shivers. Anyway, he had better tell Mrs Smyth-Fortescue. He wasn't sure whether Mrs Smyth–Fortescue would be glad or sorry that Timothy had disappeared, but she would certainly want to know.

Jeremy James stepped out of the tent and on to the lawn.

'Hello, Jeremy!' called Mrs Smyth–Fortescue through the open kitchen window. 'Did you sleep well?'

'Yes, thank you, Mrs Smyth–Forkystew,' said Jeremy James.

'I suppose Timothy's still asleep,' she said.

'I don't know,' said Jeremy James.

'You don't know?' said Mrs Smyth–Fortescue.

'Well, he's not there,' said Jeremy James.

'Not there?' echoed Mrs Smyth–Fortescue. 'Then where is he?'

'Well, we did hear a lion in the night,' said Jeremy James, 'so with a bit of luck . . .'

'Let's see if he's in his bedroom,' said Mrs Smyth–Fortescue.

So Jeremy James entered the house, and he and Mrs Smyth–Fortescue went upstairs to Timothy's bedroom. And there on the bed, totally uneaten and very asleep, lay Timothy.

'Wake up, dear!' said Mrs Smyth-Fortescue. 'Timothy, wake up!'

Timothy woke up. His eyes woke up first, and then his brain woke up second, and he sat up in surprise at the sight of his mother and Jeremy James.

'What are you doing here, dear?' asked Mrs Smyth-Fortescue. 'You were supposed to be in the tent with Jeremy.'

'Oh . . . ugh . . . um . . . er . . .' said Timothy.

'What was that, dear?' said Mrs Smyth-Fortescue.

'Um . . . ugh . . .' said Timothy.

'Why aren't you in the tent, dear?' asked Mrs Smyth-Fortescue.

Timothy looked hard at the wall. Then he looked at the floor. And then at the bed.

'Um . . . I had a tummy ache. That's it, I had a tummy ache in the night. I had a tummy ache, so I had to come in.'

'Oh, what a shame,' said Mrs Smyth-

Fortescue. 'It must have been all those sausages and beans. What a pity! And you were so looking forward to sleeping in the tent, weren't you, darling?'

'Yes, I was,' said Timothy. 'Only I had a tummy ache.'

'Well, it was very brave and sensible of you to come back here, then, dear,' said Mrs Smyth-Fortescue.

'Yes, I know,' said Timothy. 'I came back because I had a tummy ache.'

Timothy's tummy ache didn't stop him from eating a large breakfast of cornflakes, egg and bacon, and toast and marmalade. Jeremy James (who also had a large breakfast) did suggest to Timothy that perhaps people with tummy aches shouldn't be able to eat such large breakfasts, but Timothy said all campers had large breakfasts, and if Jeremy James had been a *real* camper, he'd have known that.

'A real camper,' said Jeremy James, with his mouth full of toast and marmalade, 'would know an owl isn't a ghost, and a real camper wouldn't get tummy ache in the night, and a real camper . . . a *real* camper . . .' continued Jeremy James, looking straight at Timothy, 'a *really* real camper wouldn't go to bed in his bedroom.'

Timothy munched his toast and marmalade, and for once he didn't say a word.

This story is by David Henry Wilson

Aunt Nasty

'Oh dear!' said Mother, one lunch time, after she had read a letter the postman had just left.

'What's the matter?' asked Father. Even Toby and Claire looked up from their boiled eggs.

'Aunt Nasty has written to say she is coming to stay with us,' said Mother. 'The thought of it makes me worried.'

'You must tell her we will be out!' cried Toby. He did not like the sound of Aunt Nasty.

'Or say we have no room,' said Father.

'You know I can't do that,' said Mother. 'Remember Aunt Nasty is a *witch*.'

Toby and Claire looked at each other

with round eyes. They had forgotten, for a moment, that Aunt Nasty was a witch as well as being an aunt. If they said there was no room in the house Aunt Nasty might be very cross. She might turn them into frogs.

'She is coming on the Viscount tomorrow,' said Mother, looking at the letter. 'It is hard to read this witch-writing. She writes it with a magpie's feather and all the letters look like broomsticks.'

'I see she has written it on mouse skin,' said Father.

'Isn't she just showing off?' asked Toby. 'If she was a real witch she would ride a broomstick here . . . not come on the Viscount.'

Claire had to move into Toby's room so that Aunt Nasty would have a bedroom all to herself. She put a vase of flowers in the room, but they were not garden flowers. Aunt Nasty liked flowers of a poisonous kind, like woody nightshade and foxgloves.

'Leave the cobwebs in that corner,' said Father. 'Remember how cross she was when you swept them down last time. She loves dust and cobwebs. All witches do.'

The next afternoon they went to the airport to meet Aunt Nasty. It was easy to see her in the crowd getting off the Viscount. She was one of the old sort of witch, all in black with a pointed hat and a broomstick.

'Hello, Aunt Nasty,' said Mother. 'How nice to see you again.'

'I don't suppose you are really pleased to see me,' said Aunt Nasty, 'but that doesn't matter. There is a special meeting of witches in the city this week. That is why I had to come. I will be out every night on my broom, and trying to sleep during the day. I hope the children are quiet.'

'Why didn't you come on your broom, Aunt Nasty?' asked Toby. 'Why did you have to come in the aeroplane?'

'Don't you ever listen to the weather report on the radio?' said Aunt Nasty crossly. 'It said there would be fresh winds in the Cook Strait area, increasing to gale force at midday. It isn't much fun riding a broomstick in a fresh wind let me tell you. Even the silly aeroplane bucked around. I began to think they'd put us into a wheelbarrow

73

by mistake. Two people were sick.'

'Poor people,' said Claire.

'Serve them right!' Aunt Nasty muttered. 'People with weak stomachs annoy me.'

When they got home Aunt Nasty went straight to her room. She smiled at the sight of the foxgloves and the woody nightshade, but she did not say thank you.

'I will have a cat-nap,' she said, stroking the raggy black fur collar she wore. 'I hope the bed is not damp or lumpy. I used to enjoy a damp bed when I was a young witch, but I'm getting old now.'

Then she shut the door. They heard her put her suitcase against it.

'What a rude aunt!' said Toby.

'She has to be rude, because of being a witch,' said Mother. 'Now, do be nice quiet children, won't you! Don't make her cross or she might turn you into tadpoles.'

The children went out to play, but they were not happy.

'I don't like Aunt Nasty,' said Claire.

'I don't like having a witch in the house,' said Toby.

The house was very very quiet and strange

while Aunt Nasty was there. Everyone spoke in whispery voices and went around on tiptoe. Aunt Nasty stayed in her room most of the time. Once she came out of her room and asked for some toadstools. Toby found some for her under a pine tree at the top of the hill . . . fine red ones with spots, but Aunt Nasty was not pleased with them.

'These are dreadful toadstools,' she said. 'They look good but they are disappointing. The brown, slimy ones are much better. You can't trust a boy to do anything properly these days. But I suppose I will have to make do with them.'

That was on Tuesday. Some smoke came out of the keyhole on Wednesday, and on Thursday Aunt Nasty broke a soup plate. However, they did not see her again until Friday. Then she came out and complained that there was not enough pepper in the soup.

At last it was Sunday. Aunt Nasty had been there a week. Now she was going home again – this time by broomstick. Toby and Claire were very pleased. Mother was pleased too, and yet she looked tired and sad. She went out to take some plants to the woman next door. While she was out Father came in from the garden suddenly.

'Do you know what?' he said to Toby and Claire. 'I have just remembered something. It is your mother's birthday today and we have forgotten all about it. That is what comes of having a witch in the house. We must go and buy birthday presents at once.'

'But it's Sunday, Daddy!' cried Claire. 'All the shops will be shut!'

'What on earth shall we do?' asked Father. 'There must be some way of getting a present for her.'

'A present!' said a voice. 'Who wants a present?' It was Aunt Nasty with her suitcase, a broomstick and a big black cat at her heels.

'Oh, look at the cat!' cried Claire. 'I did not know you had a cat, Aunt Nasty.'

'He sits round my neck when we ride in the bus or the plane,' said Aunt Nasty proudly. 'It is his own idea, and it is a good one, because people think he is a fur collar and I do not have to buy a ticket for him. But what is this I hear? Have you really forgotten

76

to get your mother a birthday present?'

'I'm afraid we have!' said Father sadly.

'Ha!' said Aunt Nasty fiercely. 'Now I never ever forgot my mother's birthday. I always had some little gift for her. Once I gave her the biggest blackest rat you ever saw. It was a fine rat and I would have liked it for my own pet, but nothing was too good for my mother. I let her have it.'

'I don't think Mummy would like a rat,' said Claire.

'I wasn't going to give her one!' snapped Aunt Nasty. 'Tell me, can you children draw?'

'Yes,' said Toby and Claire.

'Can you draw a birthday cake, jellies, little cakes, sandwiches, roast chickens, bottles of fizzy lemonade, balloons, crackers, pretty flowers, birds and butterflies . . . and presents too?'

'Yes!' said Toby and Claire.

'Well then, you draw them,' said Aunt Nasty, 'and I will cook up some magic. Where is the stove? Hmmm! I see it is an electric stove. It is a bit on the clean side, isn't it? An old black stove is of much more

77

use to a witch. Mind you, I've got no use for the witch who can't make do with what she can get. I will work something out, you see if I don't.'

Claire drew and Toby drew. They covered lots and lots of pages with drawings of cakes and balloons and presents wrapped in pretty paper.

Aunt Nasty came in with a smoking saucepan. 'Give me your drawings,' she said. 'Hurry up, I haven't got all day. Hmmmm! They aren't very good, are they? But they'll have to do. A good witch can manage with a scribble if she has to.'

She popped the drawings into the saucepan where they immediately caught fire and burned up to ashes. A thick blue smoke filled the room. No one could see anyone else.

'This smoke tastes like birthday cake,' called Claire.

'It tastes like jelly and ice-cream,' said Toby. The smoke began to go away up the chimney.

'I smell flowers,' said Father.

Then they saw that the whole room was changed.

Everywhere there were leaves and flowers and birds only as big as your little finger-nail. The table was covered with jellies of all colours, and little cakes and sandwiches. There was a trifle and two roasted chickens. There were huge wooden dishes of fruit – even grapes, cherries and pineapples. There was a big silver bowl of fizzy lemonade with rose petals floating in it. All around the table were presents and crackers and balloons – so many of them they would have come up to your knees.

'Aha!' said Aunt Nasty, looking pleased. 'I haven't lost my touch with a bit of pretty magic.'

Best of all was the birthday cake. It was so big there was no room for it on the table. It stood like a pink and white mountain by the fireplace. The balloons bounced and floated around the room. The tiny birds flew everywhere singing. One of them made a nest as small as a thimble in a vase of flowers.

'What is in this parcel?' asked Claire, pointing to a parcel that moved and rustled. 'Is it a rat?'

'It's two pigeons,' said Aunt Nasty. 'There is a pigeon house for them in one of the other parcels. Well, I must be off. I've wasted enough time. The saucepan is spoilt by the way, but you won't mind that. It was a nasty cheap one anyhow.'

'Won't you stay and wish Mummy a happy birthday?' asked Toby. 'She would like to say thank you for her birthday party.'

'Certainly not!' said Aunt Nasty. 'I never ever say thank you myself. I don't expect anyone to say it to me. I love rudeness, but that is because I am a witch. You are not witches, so make sure you are polite

to everybody.' She tied her suitcase to her broomstick with string and her cat climbed on to her shoulder.

'Goodbye to you anyway,' she said. 'I don't like children, but you are better than

most. Perhaps I will see you again or perhaps I won't.' She got on her broomstick and flew out of the window, her suitcase bobbing behind her. She was a bit wobbly.

'Well,' said Father, 'she wasn't so bad after all. It will be strange not having a witch in the house any more.'

'Mother will love her birthday,' said Claire. 'It was good of Aunt Nasty. It is the prettiest party I have ever seen.'

'I don't even mind if she visits us again next year,' said Toby.

'Look, there is Mummy coming now,' said Father. 'Let's go and meet her.'

They all ran out into the sunshine shouting 'Happy Birthday!' Toby had a quick look up in the air for Aunt Nasty. There, far above him, he saw a tiny little black speck that might have been Aunt Nasty or it might have been a seagull. He was not quite sure. Then he took one of Mother's hands, and Claire took the other, and they pulled her, laughing and happy, up the steps into her birthday room.

This story is by Margaret Mahy

The Tin Horseman

The weather castle was printed on a card
that hung by the window. It stood on a
rocky island in the middle of a bright blue
sea, and coloured banners flew from the tops
of its tall towers. When the weather was fair
the rocky island was blue. When rain threat-
ened the island turned purple, and when the
rain fell the island was pink.

The tin horseman lived on a shelf near the
window. He had a pale heroic face. He wore
a yellow fringed Indian suit and a headdress
of red feathers. His dapple-grey horse had
a red saddle-cloth. They had been stamped
from a sheet of tin, printed on one side only,
and shaped in a mould so that they had some
form to them.

Long ago there had been a flat tin clown, a red-and-yellow magnet, and two or three coloured rings with the horseman. Now he was alone. Day after day he looked at the little windows of the weather castle, and he was certain that he had seen the face of a beautiful yellow-haired princess at one of them.

'When the island is blue I shall gallop there and find her,' he said. But when the island was blue he did not gallop to the castle, because he was afraid.

The tin horseman was afraid of the little round yellow glass-topped box that was the monkey game of skill. Inside it crouched the monkey, printed on a yellow background. He had a horrid pink face, and empty holes where his eyes belonged. His eyes were silver balls that had to be shaken into place. The tin horseman was afraid that when the monkey had his eyes in place he might do dreadful things, and he was sure that the monkey was skilful enough to shake them into place whenever he wanted to. The monkey lived between the tin horseman and

the castle, and the tin horseman never dared
to gallop past.

Day after day he looked at the castle
windows, and daily he became more certain
that he saw the yellow-haired princess. Once
he thought she even waved her hand to him.
'When the island is pink I shall gallop there,'
he said. 'One rainy day I shall smash the glass
and throw away the monkey's silver eyes and
ride to the princess.' But he was afraid, and
stayed where he was, dusty on the shelf.

One night, just between midnight and the
twelve strokes of the clock, words came to

the tin horseman: 'Now or never.' He didn't know whether he had heard them or thought them, but his fear left him, and in the dim light from the window he spurred his horse towards the weather castle and the princess of his dreams.

Just as he was passing the monkey game of skill he was surrounded by complete darkness. All was black, and he could see nothing. Again words came to him: 'Fear is blind, but courage gives me eyes.' And again the tin horseman did not know where the words came from nor why he did what he did next.

He dismounted, and felt in the dark for the monkey game of skill. He remembered his thought of smashing the glass and throwing away the eyes, but he did not do that. He shook it gently. One, two, he heard the eyes roll into place. He closed his eyes and waited. A golden glow came from the glass top of the box, and seeing the glow through his closed eyelids he opened his eyes. The monkey was gone. There in the golden light stood the yellow-haired princess he had longed for. She was not in the weather castle, but here before him.

'Your courage has broken my enchant-
ment,' she said. 'There is a sorcerer who
lives in the weather castle. It was he who
wanted you to smash the glass and throw
away the monkey's eyes, and if you had
done that I should have been lost to you
for ever.'

'Now I *will* ride to the castle,' said the
tin horseman. He prised the glass top off the
box and took the princess up on his horse.

Over the blue sea they galloped, straight to the island and across the drawbridge to the castle. The castle was empty. The sorcerer had fled.

After that the tin horseman and the princess lived in the weather castle with the coloured banners flying from the towers, while the island turned blue or pink or purple as the weather changed.

But the glass was back on top of the little round yellow box that had been the monkey game of skill. From then on someone else lived there, and no one ever looked to see who it might be.

This story is by Russell Hoban

The Man Who Rode the Tiger

Once there was a tiger, a fierce tiger. One day, when the wind blew and the rain fell down and there was thunder and lightning, the tiger crept close to the wall of a little house in a village, trying to get some shelter. If he pressed close enough, the wind and the rain would not soak him so much; so he pressed very close and flat.

Now inside the house an old woman was shouting angrily. The roof of the little house was full of holes and the rain was coming in, soaking the furniture, and the old woman was scurrying about trying to push everything out of the way of the drips. 'Oh,' she shouted. 'This perpetual dripping! It's driving me mad!' And she gave another shout, and another wail, as more water came through. 'Oh this perpetual dripping! It's driving me mad! Two or three days of peace and quiet, that's all. Then the perpetual dripping gets me again!'

The tiger, hearing her shouts, became very frightened of the Perpetual Dripping. He had never seen a Perpetual Dripping, never even heard of one. 'It must be an enormous monster,' he thought. 'Much bigger and fiercer than a tiger. How she screams!' If it hadn't been pouring so hard, he would have run away at once, for fear the Perpetual Dripping would get him too.

As it was, he pressed close to the wall, with the storm crashing about on one side of him, and the woman's shouting on the other, wondering which he was afraid of more, the wind and the rain, or the Perpetual Dripping. And every time the woman dragged some furniture across the floor, to get it out of the way of the drips, he listened to the slithering, banging, rumbling sound, and he shook in all his four legs, and he thought, 'That is the roar of the Perpetual Dripping. I hope it doesn't get me.'

Well, while he was pressed so wretchedly against the wall, a man came along. Now the man was looking for his donkey, who had been frightened by the thunder and lightning, and had run away. In the lightning flash, he saw a large animal near the wall of the hut, and he thought it was his donkey. In lightning, you know, it is light one minute and dark the next, and you cannot see very well. He rushed up to the tiger and grabbed it by one ear, and started to scold it. 'You bad beast, you! You bad beast! Making me trudge all round in the storm! Getting me soaking wet!' And he pulled a stick from his belt and started to hit the tiger, shouting all the time.

The tiger had never been treated like this before. No one had ever grabbed him by the ear, let alone hit him. 'Goodness!' he thought. 'It's the Perpetual Dripping! It's got me too!' And he was terribly frightened.

The man pushed him and shoved him and dragged him along. The tiger didn't dare fight back, but came along as meekly as you please, because he thought it was the Perpetual Dripping. 'No wonder the old woman was frightened,' he said to himself. 'It *is* terrible.'

Then the man got on the tiger's back and made the tiger carry him home, kicking him and hitting him and shouting at him the whole time without stopping; and the tiger was very frightened. At last they reached the house, and the old man tied the tiger up to a post in front of the door and went to bed. All the rest of the night, the tiger stood shivering, thinking, 'I hope the Perpetual Dripping doesn't come back for a bit. I hope I have two or three days of peace, like the old woman said.'

Now in the morning the man's wife went out and she nearly jumped out of her skin when she saw a tiger fastened to the front door. 'Do you know what you brought home last night?' she shouted to her husband.

'Of course I do!' he shouted back. 'That wretched donkey.'

'Funny-looking donkey,' she said. 'Come and see.'

The old man grumbled because he hadn't had much sleep, but he pulled on his trousers and came to have a look. And when he saw what he had really brought home last night and had tied so firmly to the front door, he fell flat on his face and couldn't be persuaded to look again till dinner-time.

Now somehow or other – you know how one person tells another – the news spread around that this man had actually ridden on a tiger. The King came to see. When he saw that the story was true, he gave the man bags of money so that he could dress in silk and live in a beautiful house and *look* like a man who rode on a tiger. Then the King went back to his palace again, very pleased.

But one day some enemy soldiers came riding against the King. There were so many of them, that the King didn't know what to do. 'I will send for the man who rode on a tiger!' he said. 'Such a man will make mincemeat of them!' So he sent a message to the man, and together with the message he sent a huge, fierce horse for the man to come galloping to the rescue.

When the man received the message – and the horse – he was terrified. 'Now I'm in a pickle!' he said to his wife. 'I've got to help the King! I've got to drive away all the enemy soldiers! I've got to ride this horse! I've never even sat on a horse in my life, you know I haven't! And look at this one, rolling its eyes at me!'

'Don't make such a fuss,' said his wife. 'You only need practice. Just get on.'

'Just get on!' he said. 'Just get on! Would you mind telling me how I do it?'

'Jump!' said his wife.

So the man started to jump. He jumped and he jumped, but he never seemed to jump anywhere near the top of the horse.

'You'll have to jump higher,' said his wife.

'Have to jump higher!' said the man, to nobody in particular.

Still he started to jump higher, but that was no better either. All that happened was that he fell on his nose.

'The trouble is,' said the man, 'when I jump I get muddled; because I can't remember which way to turn, and that makes me fall over.'

'The way to turn,' said his wife, 'is the way that will make your face come near the horse's face.'

'Yes, that's it,' said the man, and he jumped again, and this time he was actually on the horse's back. But his face was near the horse's tail.

'No, no!' said his wife. And he had to fall off again.

So he tried and he tried, jumping and falling, and pulling and scrabbling, and getting all tangled up with the stirrups and the reins and the horse's tail. Then just as he had decided he had had enough, he suddenly found himself sitting on the horse's back.

'Quick!' he shouted. 'Tie me on before I fall off again!'

His wife dashed up with some ropes, and quickly she tied his feet to the stirrups and then tied the stirrups under the horse, quickly she tied a rope round his waist and fastened that to the saddle, quickly she tied a rope round his shoulders and tied that to the horse's neck, quickly she tied a rope round the man's neck and tied that to the horse's tail.

By this time the horse was getting nervous, wondering what was happening to him, and he started to run. The man shouted, 'Wife, wife! You haven't tied my hands! They're loose!'

'Fasten them into the horse's mane!' she shouted after him. And as the horse gained ground and galloped faster, the man wound the horse's mane round his hands, and held on for dear life.

They went this way and that, over fields and fences and streams and walls, kicking

up the dust behind them. The wind whistled past the man's ears and his nose grew
red.

'You're taking me right to those enemy
soldiers!' he shouted. 'Whoa, whoa! I'm not
going, I tell you!' He took one of his hands
out of the horse's mane and grabbed at a
little tree, thinking to stop the horse. But
the horse was going so fast, and the earth

that the little tree was growing in was so soft from all the rains, that the tree came up in his hand and there he was thundering along on this fierce horse, brandishing a tree in his hand.

When the enemy soldiers saw him galloping towards them like that, they were very frightened. 'Did you see!' they shouted to each other. 'He pulled up a tree to hit us with! A whole tree! This is certainly the man who rode on a tiger.' And they ran for their lives and were never seen again.

Just at that moment, the horse stopped dead, the ropes all snapped, and the man fell off the horse's back. But luckily there was no one to see.

When the man had recovered his breath, he walked home, leading the horse by the bridle. He preferred it that way, because nothing on earth, he said out loud, would ever induce him to get on a horse again. And when the people saw him coming, they said, 'What a wonderful man he is! He drove away the enemy soldiers all by himself, and instead of showing off like another man would, riding splendidly on his tiger or galloping on his fierce horse, he comes back walking on his own two legs like a perfectly ordinary person, just as if he wasn't brave at all!'

This story is by Leila Berg

The Riddlemaster

Sitting on one of the public benches in the High Street one warm Saturday morning, Polly licked all round the top of an ice-cream horn.

A large person sat down suddenly beside her. The bench swayed and creaked, and Polly looked round.

'Good morning, Wolf!'

'Good morning, Polly.'

'Nice day, Wolf.'

'Going to be hot, Polly.'

'Mmm,' Polly said. She was engaged in trying to save a useful bit of ice-cream with her tongue before it dripped on to the pavement and was wasted.

'In fact it is hot now, Polly.'

'I'm not too hot,' Polly said.
'Perhaps that delicious-looking ice is cool-ing you down,' the wolf said enviously.

'Perhaps it is,' Polly agreed.

'I'm absolutely boiling,' the wolf said.

Polly fished in the pocket of her cotton dress and pulled out a threepenny bit. It was more than half what she had left, but she was a kind girl, and in a way she was fond of the wolf, tiresome as he sometimes was.

'Here you are, Wolf,' she said, holding it out to him. 'Go into Woolworths and get one for yourself.'

There was a scurry of feet, a flash of black fur, and a little cloud of white summer dust rose off the pavement near Polly's feet. The wolf had gone.

Two minutes later he came back, a good deal more slowly. He was licking his ice-cream horn with a very long red tongue and it was disappearing extremely quickly. He sat down again beside Polly with a satisfied grunt.

'Mm! Just what I needed. Thank you very much, Polly.'

'Not at all, Wolf,' said Polly, who had thought that he might have said this before.

She went on licking her ice in a happy dream-like state, while the wolf did the same, but twice as fast.

Presently, in a slightly aggrieved voice, the wolf said, 'Haven't you nearly finished?'

'Well no, not nearly,' Polly said. She always enjoyed spinning out ices as long as possible. 'Have you?'

'Ages ago.'

'I wish you wouldn't look at me so hard, Wolf,' Polly said, wriggling. 'It makes me feel uncomfortable when I'm eating.'

'I was only thinking,' the wolf said.

'You look sad, then, when you think,' Polly remarked.

'I generally am. It's a very sad world, Polly.'

'Is it?' said Polly, in surprise.

'Yes. A lot of sad things happen.'

'What things?' asked Polly.

'Well, I finish up all my ice-cream.'

'That's fairly sad. But at any rate you did have it,' Polly said.

'I haven't got it Now,' the wolf said. 'And it's Now that I want it. Now is the only time to eat ice-cream.'

'When you are eating it, it is Now,' Polly remarked.

'But when I'm not, it isn't. I wish it was always Now,' the wolf sighed.

'It sounds like a riddle,' Polly said.

'What does?'

'What you were saying. When is Now not Now or something like that. You know the sort I mean – when is a door not a door?'

'I love riddles,' said the wolf in a much more cheerful voice. 'I know lots. Let's ask each other riddles.'

'Yes, let's,' said Polly.

'And I tell you what would make it really amusing. Let's say that whoever wins can eat the other person up.'

'Wins how?' Polly asked, cautiously.

'By asking three riddles the other person can't answer.'

'Three in a row,' Polly insisted.

'Very well. Three in a row.'

'And I can stop whenever I want to.'

'All right,' the wolf agreed, unwillingly. 'And I'll start,' he added quickly. 'What made the penny stamp?'

Polly knew it was because the threepenny

105

bit, and said so. Then she asked the wolf what made the apple turnover, and he knew the answer to that. Polly knew what was the longest word in the dictionary, and the wolf knew what has an eye but cannot see. This reminded him of the question of what has hands, but no fingers and a face, but no nose, to which Polly was able to reply that it was a clock.

'My turn,' she said, with relief. 'Wolf, what gets bigger, the more you take away from it?'

The wolf looked puzzled.

'Are you sure you've got it right, Polly?' he asked at length. 'You don't mean it gets smaller the more you take away from it?'

'No, I don't.'

'It gets bigger?'

'Yes.'

'No cake I ever saw did that,' the wolf said, thinking aloud. 'Some special kind of pudding, perhaps?'

'It's not a pudding,' Polly said.

'I know!' the wolf said triumphantly. 'It's the sort of pain you get when you're hungry. And the more you don't eat the

worse the pain gets. That's getting bigger
the less you do about it.'

'No, you're wrong,' Polly said. 'It isn't
a pain or anything to eat, either. It's a hole.
The more you take away, the bigger it gets,
don't you see, Wolf?'

'Being hungry is a sort of hole in your
inside,' the wolf said. 'But anyhow it's my
turn now. I'm going to ask you a new riddle, so you won't know the answer already,
and I don't suppose you'll be able to guess
it, either. What gets filled up three or four
times a day, and yet can always hold more?'

'Do you mean it can hold more after
it's been filled?' Polly asked.

The wolf thought, and then said, 'Yes.'

'But it couldn't, Wolf! If it was really
properly filled up it couldn't hold any more.'

'It does though,' the wolf said triumphantly. 'It seems to be quite bursting full
and then you try very hard and it still holds
a little more.'

Polly had her suspicions of what this
might be, but she didn't want to say in
case she was wrong.

'I can't guess.'

'It's me!' the wolf cried, in delight. 'Got you, that time, Polly! However full up I am, I can always manage a little bit more. Your turn next, Polly.'

'What,' Polly said, 'is the difference between an elephant and a pillar-box?'

The wolf thought for some time.

'The elephant is bigger,' he said, at last.

'Yes. But that isn't the right answer.'

'The pillar-box is red. Bright red. And the elephant isn't.'

'Ye-es. But that isn't the right answer either.'

The wolf looked puzzled. He stared hard at the old-fashioned Victorian pillar-box in the High Street. It had a crimped lid with a knob on top like a silver teapot. But it didn't help him. After some time he said crossly, 'I don't know.'

'You mean you can't tell the difference between an elephant and a pillar-box?'

'No.'

'Then I shan't send you to post my letters,' Polly said, triumphantly. She thought this was a very funny riddle.

The wolf, however, didn't.

'You don't see the joke, Wolf?' Polly asked, a little disappointed that he was so unmoved.

'I see it, yes. But I don't think it's funny. It's not a proper riddle at all. It's just silly.'

'Now you ask me something,' Polly suggested. After a minute or two's thought, the wolf said, 'What is the difference between pea soup and a clean pocket handkerchief?'

'Pea soup is hot and a pocket handkerchief is cold,' said Polly.

'No. Anyhow you could have cold pea soup.'

'Pea soup is green,' said Polly.

'I expect a clean pocket handkerchief could be green too, if it tried,' said the wolf. 'Do you give it up?'

'Well,' said Polly, 'of course I do know the difference, but I don't know what you want me to say.'

'I want you to say you don't know the difference between them,' said the wolf, crossly.

'But I do,' said Polly.

'But then I can't say what I was going to say!' the wolf cried.

He looked so much disappointed that Polly relented.

'All right, then, you say it.'

'You don't know the difference between pea soup and a clean pocket handkerchief?'

'I'll pretend I don't. No, then,' said Polly. 'You ought to be more careful what you keep in your pockets,' the wolf said. He laughed so much at this that he choked, and Polly had to beat him hard on the back before he recovered and could sit back comfortably on the seat again.

'Your turn,' he said, as soon as he could speak.

Polly thought carefully. She thought of a riddle about a man going to St Ives; of one about the man who showed a portrait to another man; of one about a candle; but she was not satisfied with any of them. With so many riddles it isn't really so much a question of guessing the answers, as of knowing them or not knowing them already, and if the wolf were to invent a completely new riddle out of his head, he would be able to eat her, Polly, in no time at all.

'Hurry up,' said the wolf.

Perhaps it was seeing his long red tongue at such very close quarters or it may have been the feeling that she had no time to lose, that made Polly say, before she had considered what she was going to say, 'What is it that has teeth, but no mouth?'

'Grrr,' said the wolf, showing all his teeth for a moment. 'Are you quite sure he hasn't a mouth, Polly?'

'Quite sure. And I'm supposed to be asking the questions, not you, Wolf.'

The wolf did not appear to hear this. He had now turned his back on Polly and was going through some sort of rapid repetition in a subdued gabble, through which Polly could hear only occasional words.

'. . . Grandma, so I said the better to see you with, gabble, gabble, gabble, Ears you've got, gabble gabble better to hear gabble gabble gabble gabble gabble TEETH gabble eat you all up.'

He turned round with a satisfied air.

'I've guessed it, Polly. It's a GRAND-MOTHER.'

'No,' said Polly astonished.

'Well then, Red Riding Hood's grandmother if you are so particular. The story mentions her eyes and her ears and her teeth, so I expect she hadn't got anything else. No mouth anyhow.'

'It's not anyone's grandmother.'

'Not a grandmother,' said the wolf slowly. He shook his head. 'It's difficult. Tell me some more about it. Are they sharp teeth, Polly?'

'They can be,' Polly said.

'As sharp as mine?' asked the wolf, showing his for comparison.

'No,' said Polly, drawing back a little. 'But more tidily arranged,' she added.

The wolf shut his jaws with a snap.

'I give up,' he said, in a disagreeable tone. 'There isn't anything I know of that has teeth and no mouth. What use would the teeth be to anyone without a mouth? I mean, what is the point of taking a nice juicy bite out of something if you've got to find someone else's mouth to swallow it for you? It doesn't make sense.'

'It's a comb,' said Polly, when she got a chance to speak.

'A what?' cried the wolf in disgust.

'A COMB. What you do your hair with. It's got teeth, hasn't it? But no mouth. A comb, Wolf.'

The wolf looked sulky. Then he said in a bright voice, 'My turn now, and I'll begin straight away. What is the difference between a nice fat young pink pig and a plate of sausages and bacon? You don't know, of course, so I'll tell you. It's— '

'Wolf!' Polly interrupted.

'It's a very good riddle, this one, and I can't blame you for not having guessed it. The answer is— '

'WOLF!' Polly said, 'I want to tell you something.'

'Not the answer?'

'No. Not the answer. Something else.'

'Well, go on.'

'Look, Wolf, we made a bargain, didn't we, that whoever lost three lives running by not being able to answer riddles, might be eaten up by the other person?'

'Yes,' the wolf agreed. 'And you've lost two already, and now you're not going to be able to answer the third and then I shall eat you up. Now I'll tell you what

the difference is between a nice fat little
pink— '

'NO!' Polly shouted. 'Listen, Wolf! I
may have lost two lives already, but you
have lost three!'

'I haven't!'

'Yes, you have! You couldn't answer the
riddle about the hole, you didn't know the
difference between an elephant and a pillar-
box— '

'I do!' said the wolf indignantly.

'Well, you may now, but you didn't
when I asked you the riddle; and you didn't
know about the comb having teeth and no
mouth. That was three you couldn't answer
in a row, so it isn't you that is going to eat
me up.'

'What is it then?' the wolf asked, shaken.

'It's me that is going to eat you up!'
said Polly.

The wolf moved rather further away.

'Are you really going to eat me up, Polly?'

'In a moment, Wolf. I'm just considering
how I'll have you cooked,' said Polly.

'I'm very tough, Polly.'

'That's all right, Wolf. I can simmer you gently over a low flame until you are tender.'

'I don't suppose I'd fit very nicely into any of your saucepans, Polly.'

'I can use the big one Mother has for making jam. That's an enormous saucepan,' said Polly, thoughtfully, measuring the wolf with her eyes.

The wolf began visibly to shake where he sat.

'Oh please, Polly, don't eat me. Don't eat me up this time,' he urged. 'Let me off this once, I promise I'll never do it again.'

'Never do what again?' Polly asked.

'I don't know. What was I doing?' the wolf asked himself, in despair.

'Trying to get me to eat,' Polly suggested.

'Well, of course, I'm always doing that,' the wolf agreed.

'And you would have eaten me?' Polly asked.

'Not if you'd asked very nicely, I wouldn't,' the wolf said. 'Like I'm asking now.'

'And if I didn't eat you up, you'd stop trying to get me?'

The wolf considered.

'Look,' he said, 'I can't say I'll stop for ever, because after all a wolf is a wolf, and if I promised to stop for ever I wouldn't be a wolf any more. But I promise to stop for a long time. I won't try any more today.'

'And what about after today?' Polly insisted.

'The first time I catch you,' the wolf said dreamily, 'if you ask *very* nicely I'll

116

let you go because you've let me off today. But after that, no mercy! It'll be just Snap! Crunch! Swallow!'

'All right,' Polly said, recollecting that so far the wolf had not ever got as far as catching her successfully even once. 'You can go.'

The wolf ducked his head gratefully and trotted off. Polly saw him threading his way between the busy shoppers in the High Street.

But she sat contentedly in the hot sun and wondered what was the difference between a fat pink pig and a plate of sausages and bacon. Not much, if she knew her wolf!

This story is by Catherine Storr

Odysseus and Circe

Odysseus and his men sailed on, caring only to reach their homes on the isle of Ithaca. When there was a good breeze, they hoisted the sails and sped over the blue waves. When there was no wind, they bent their backs to the oars and pulled sturdily. The voyage was long and weary. They had many times been driven off their course, and Odysseus decided to ask for the help of the god Aeolus, in whose keeping were all the winds that blow. So he steered his ship towards the island where Aeolus lived, and the other ships followed. Next day they put in at the harbour, and Odysseus went up to the palace of King Aeolus. The King and his family were feasting. The traveller was hospitably entertained, and next morning Aeolus gave him a leather bag whose mouth was tied with a thong. It bulged with all the winds. Odysseus was told to release only the west wind, and this would drive his ship home. He thanked the King, rejoined his men, weighed anchor and set off. He kept the bag beside him, and himself managed the helm. Then he carefully opened the bulging bag and let out only the west wind. Gradually the sails filled, and the ship bounded over the waves.

For several days the ship rode on. Odysseus alone managed the helm, so fearful was he that they might go off course. At length he became weary and, almost within sight of his native land, he lay down on the deck and fell fast asleep. The moon came out and shone on the sleeping form of the leader and on the bulging leather bag he kept beside him.

The sailors gathered round and began talking in undertones.

'I'd like to know what the old man has in that bag,' said one of them.

'Mark my words,' said another, 'that

King – Aeolus, wasn't it? – gave him some treasure to take home, and that's what's in the bag.'

'Yes, shouldn't wonder. He's going to keep it all to himself. We'll ask him for a share of it.'

'First, let's look inside and make sure what it is. Gold and silver and precious stones, I shouldn't wonder.'

'Come on then. Undo the bag. Do it quietly or you'll wake him.'

Then the sailor nearest to Odysseus drew out a sharp knife and cut the cord that bound the neck of the bag. Instantly all the other winds rushed out with a mighty roar, and Odysseus awoke to find the ship tossing madly in all directions.

'Fools!' he cried. 'What have you done? You have ruined everything, and we shall be destroyed by storms. Quick, lower the sails. Get to your stations and man the oars.'

But it was too late. Already the sails were filled with a great wind from the north-east. The ship rocked and pitched. The men had strength only to lower the smaller of the sails. They were driven violently back towards the island of Aeolus, which they had left only a few days earlier.

Odysseus made the men take the ship into harbour, and once more he sought the help of Aeolus. But the King spoke to him sternly.

'No,' he said. 'I dare not help you further. The gods are against you. This is proved by your falling asleep when at the helm and allowing your men to act recklessly. You must continue your journey without my help.'

Once more they set out, but now the winds failed and the sails hung idly, flapping against the masts. The men were obliged to use the oars. At length, weary and discouraged, they put in at the island of the Laestrygonians in search of food and water. These were a race of cannibal giants, as savage and barbarous as the Cyclopes. Some of the ships went right into the harbour, but Odysseus wisely remained in open water outside. As soon as the giants saw the ships, they seized the great rocks and hurled them over the cliffs, smashing two or three of the ships to fragments. As rock after rock crashed down on the decks, the sailors could do nothing except scramble into the water and make for the shore as best they could. Here the cruel Laestrygonians speared them from above, so that none was left alive. Seeing that he could do nothing to help them, Odysseus gave orders to his crew to row for their lives and get as far away as possible from the accursed island.

In course of time the ship reached the island of Aeaea, where lived the enchantress Circe, bright-haired daughter of the sun. Here on the shore Odysseus and his men rested for two days. There was no sign of life on the island, so Odysseus climbed a high hill not far inland to spy out the country. He saw no human habitations except one. This was a fair palace standing in a glade among trees in the centre of the island. He returned to the shore and told his men what he had discovered. Then he divided the party into two – one under his own command, the other under the command of Eurylochus. The two leaders drew lots as to which should go first and make himself known at the palace. The lot fell to Eurylochus, who with his men set off towards the centre of the island. Odysseus and his party awaited their return.

When Eurylochus and his men reached the grove where stood the palace, they were surrounded by lions and wolves. In terror some of them turned to run. Others drew their spears and prepared to fight. But to their amazement the beasts were all tame, fawning upon them and licking their hands and faces, as a dog greets his master after a long absence.

The reason was this. The beasts had all been men, but they had been changed by the magic power of the enchantress Circe. They had the forms of lions and wolves, but their hearts and minds were still those of men.

Encouraged by this, the party approached the gates of the palace. Within they heard the sound of sweet music and of women's voices. Then the bright-haired queen herself came out and beckoned them inside. All went in except Eurylochus. He was afraid and waited outside the gate.

Circe bade the men be seated at a long table in her hall. Then she had servants place before them delicate food and strong wine. The men feasted and drank as they had never done before. As they did so, Circe walked back and forth before her great loom, weaving a cloth of rich dyes and mysterious design, singing to herself in her high, unearthly voice.

Then, when she saw that her guests were half asleep with eating and drinking, she took up a golden wand of delicate work-manship and touched each of them lightly on the shoulder, muttering an incantation in some strange tongue. Instantly each of the sailors was turned into a pig. Grunting and jostling each other, they ran about the hall. Their flapping ears, bristly skins and curved tusks were those of pigs, but their hearts and minds remained their own. Circe summoned her swineherds who, with sharp sticks drove the squealing beasts into sties at the rear of the palace. Here they were penned in and fed on beechnuts and acorns and the swill from the kitchens.

Seeing all this, Eurylochus, in fear and sorrow, sped back to the shore to tell their leader what had happened.

'Where are your companions?' asked Odysseus as soon as he saw Eurylochus. 'What has become of my men?'

'Oh master,' cried Eurylochus with tears in his eyes, 'a terrible thing has befallen them!' Then with horror and despair making his tale more piteous, he described all he had seen.

At once Odysseus set off alone to see what he could do to deliver his men from their terrible captivity. In vain Eurylochus pleaded with him not to go, or at least to take some trusted companion. But Odysseus, as brave as he was cunning, set off alone.

Halfway to the palace he met a young man of pleasing appearance who greeted him and begged speech with him.

'You are the famous Odysseus, I know,' said the youth, 'and you are on your way home after serving the Greeks at Troy.'

Then the young man said he was Hermes, messenger of the gods, who had bidden him find out Odysseus and be of service to him in his journey.

'Circe,' he told Odysseus, 'is an enchantress of great power and she has changed your men into beasts, just as you have been told. She will do the same to you, and I advise you to get as far from her as you can and put as many sea miles as possible between you and her island.'

'No,' said Odysseus firmly. 'I brought the men here, and it is for me to do what I can to rescue them.'

'Very well,' said Hermes. 'Since you are determined to face the enchantress, listen to me carefully. Gather some of this herb you see growing about you – the one with the black root and the white flower, called moly. Keep it with you when you encounter the witch, and it will protect you against her enchantments. When she attempts to bewitch you, you must rush at her with your sword drawn and make as if to cut her throat. When she is at your mercy, she will agree to do all you ask. Now do as I say, and may the gods protect you.'

Odysseus thanked the young man and went on his way. He boldly entered the courtyard of the palace and stood before the entrance. Circe, the bright-haired daughter of the sun god, her heart dark with mischief,

welcomed him in and treated him court-
eously, bidding him be seated at her table.
Servants brought him food and wine, and
she entertained him by singing before her
loom. Then, when he had feasted and drunk,
she stepped swiftly towards him, touched
him on the shoulder with her golden wand
and said in a shrill, inhuman voice:

'There, stranger! Now go to the sty and
eat with your fellow-swine!'

But Odysseus grew no long bristles,
nor did he grunt and squeal. Instead, he
drew his sharp sword, brandished it over
the enchantress and stared into her face with
a look of fury. The sorceress was beaten. She
went down on her knees, raised her hands
towards him and begged to be allowed to
live.

'Very well,' said Odysseus. 'On one
condition. Repeat after me this oath.'

Then she swore to restore Odysseus's
companions to their former manly shape,
entertain them hospitably and without doing
them further harm, and finally let them go in
peace and security.

'You are Odysseus,' she said when she

had sworn the oath. 'Hermes came and told me to expect you. I will release your sailors and you shall all be entertained at my palace for as long as you wish to stay.'

At once the men who had been turned into pigs were changed back into men. They looked even younger and more handsome than before. Odysseus went back to the shore to summon the others to the palace. Eurylochus was still afraid and wished to remain behind, but Odysseus would not let him.

'Come,' he said. 'All is now safe. Let us eat and drink at the queen's expense and pass our days in ease and pleasure.'

Circe did all that she had promised. Odysseus and his men were royally entertained, and for many days they stayed with her. They roamed the island, playing games amongst themselves or swimming in the blue sea as if they had no cares in the world. They feasted and drank to their hearts' content, and Circe practised no further enchantments upon them. It seemed as if Odysseus had forgotten his home and the purpose of his voyage.

At last Eurylochus and some of the others reminded him that they had wives and children who had been waiting for their return for many long years. Odysseus agreed to bid farewell to the enchantress. She parted from him with tears of farewell in her eyes, giving him instructions for the next stage of his journey. In particular she warned him of the dangers that awaited him when he should pass the island of the Sirens. Then one bright morning when the wind was favourable, Odysseus made sacrifice to the gods and boarded his ship. The men hoisted sail, weighed anchor and watched the island of Aeaea grow smaller in the distance.

Not long afterwards Odysseus knew that the ship was approaching the Sirens, so he ordered everything to be done as Circe had advised. The island, he was told, was surrounded by treacherous and jagged rocks, on which a ship might be wrecked and a swimmer torn to pieces. On the shores of this island lay the Sirens, maidens of great beauty not unlike the mermaids of later legends. As they combed their long flowing hair, they sang songs of such unearthly sweetness that no man who heard them could resist their magic. Some played on stringed instruments made from great sea-shells. All raised their voices in strains of unrivalled harmony, not heard elsewhere by human ears. Many was the good ship which had been steered on to the rocks by men unable to sail past the Sirens' island; many were the young sailors who had leaped into the sea and been torn to pieces on the hidden rocks, so that whitening bones and fragments of wreckage were to be seen all along the shore as a warning to desperate and foolish mariners. Those relics should have spoken plainly to all, but Circe had urged Odysseus to take no risks.

He told the men to fill their ears with wax, so that they should not hear the song of the Sirens. As for him, he stood with his back to the mainmast and his eyes towards the shore, while his men bound him to the mast with ropes. On no account were they to obey him if he should tell them to release him. He was to remain bound to the mast so long as the island was within sight and sound.

No sooner were these preparations complete than they came in sight of the shore, edged with the bones of sailors and tall ships. On the beaches lay the Sirens, some combing their hair, others plucking the strings of their lyres. All sang. The mariners saw everything but heard nothing. Their leader alone was allowed to listen to the ravishing strains of their music, as they beckoned to him with song and gesture to come and taste the joys of their island. He was seized with an overwhelming desire to sail nearer. Sweating and straining, he heaved at the ropes till they cut into his flesh and he cried out in pain. Then he signalled to the men to come and cut the cords. But they obeyed his earlier command and brought more ropes to lash him still faster to the mast. It seemed as if the mast would crack with the strain. Then at last, out of breath from his exertions, he relaxed and leaned back, his ears filled with the Sirens' music, till it grew fainter and fainter as the ship swung past the fatal shore and the gleaming beaches, and the maidens and their songs were lost in the distance.

When the place was no more than a speck
on the horizon, Odysseus ordered the crew
to release him and take the wax from their
ears. Thus one more danger was passed on
the long voyage back to Ithaca from the
ruined city of Troy.

This retelling of the legend of Odysseus
and Circe is by James Reeves

The Three Wishes

In the days when there were fairies, it was sensible to take care. A bit of foolishness which offended the fairies meant a great deal of trouble. On the other hand, if you made a friend of one of them – ah well! – then you were in luck.

A poor farm labourer was finishing his day's work when he saw a commotion in a gorse bush. He ran over to it and, in the centre, he saw a little woman, stuck fast. She was quite old but no bigger than a tiny child. She was struggling and kicking and making no progress. And what a noise she was making! Such language! I shall not describe it. The man quickly took hold of the prickly branches and forced them apart.

Then, gently, he helped the fairy woman to safety.

'Well,' she said briskly, pulling the prickles from her clothes, 'that was well done, mortal man.'

'Not at all, madam, my pleasure,' said the man carefully because he knew about fairies.

'You shall be rewarded,' she said. 'Are you married?'

'Yes, madam.'

'Are you rich?'

The man laughed.

'We are very poor,' he answered, 'but happy.'

'Indeed? You are fortunate, but a little wealth will do you no harm. I have decided. I shall grant your wife three wishes.'

The man bowed low, but when he looked up again she had vanished.

The man hurried home to his cottage where his wife had made up the fire, but there was little to cook on it.

'Have you brought something for supper?' asked the wife.

'Better than that,' he replied. 'Just wait until I tell you! I met a fairy in the Long Field today and she has granted you three wishes. Be careful, wife. What will you wish for first? Let us think about it.'

'What nonsense,' snorted his wife, who was hungry. 'If I had a wish, I'd wish for a good, fat sausage.'

No sooner had she wished, than there was a slithering noise, and a frying pan slid down the chimney and sat neatly on the fire.

In the pan, coiled round and round, was a wonderful sausage. A delicious smell filled the air as it began to cook. The wife was astonished and delighted but the husband was not so pleased.

'You must wish for something sensible,' he said. 'A sausage is all very well for now, but what of our future? You could have wished for a farm, or a chest full of jewels.' He poked the pan irritably and it overturned and the sausage fell in the ashes.

'Look what you've done,' shrieked his wife. 'That lovely sausage! Our supper! I wish that sausage was stuck on your stupid nose!'

No sooner had she wished, than there was a slithering noise and the sausage attached itself to the man's nose and hung there. He felt it carefully, but there was no doubt. It was part of his nose.

'I'll cut it off,' cried his wife, seizing the carving knife.

'No, no,' groaned the man, 'it will be like cutting off my nose. It's stuck there for ever. Whatever shall I do? I can't blow my sausage, can I? This is terrible, a disaster.'

The wife began to cry, regretting her hasty wish, while the man stood and squinted down the sausage, wondering what to do.

'There's only one way out,' he decided. 'You must wish the sausage back in the pan.'

'But the farm, the jewels? I have only one more wish.' The wife wailed and the husband argued, though it was difficult enough with a fine, fat sausage on his nose. At last she was persuaded, and she made her third wish. With a slithering noise, the sausage flew back into the pan. The delicious smell returned as the sausage sizzled and the man looked as he had always looked. Not handsome, you understand, but better than with a sausage on his nose.

So they remained poor, but they also remained happy, so that is not so bad, is it?

This is a retelling of the traditional tale by Pat Thomson

Mr Pepperpot Buys Macaroni

'It's a very long time since we've had macaroni for supper,' said Mr Pepperpot one day.

'Then you shall have it today, my love,' said his wife. 'But I shall have to go to the grocer for some. So first of all you'll have to find me.'

'Find you?' said Mr Pepperpot. 'What sort of nonsense is that?' But when he looked round for her he couldn't see her anywhere. 'Don't be silly, wife,' he said; 'if you're hiding in the cupboard you must come out this minute. We're too big to play hide-and-seek.'

'*I'm* not too big, I'm just the right size for "hunting-the-pepperpot",' laughed Mrs Pepperpot. 'Find me if you can!'

'I'm not going to charge round my own bedroom looking for my wife,' he said crossly.

'Now, now! I'll help you; I'll tell you when you're warm. Just now you're very cold.' For Mr Pepperpot was peering out of the window, thinking she might have jumped out. As he searched round the room she called out 'Warm!' 'Colder!' 'Getting hotter!' until he was quite dizzy.

At last she shouted, 'You'll burn the top of your bald head if you don't look up!' And there she was, sitting on the bedpost, swinging her legs and laughing at him.

Her husband pulled a very long face when he saw her. 'This is a bad business – a very bad business,' he said, stroking her cheek with his little finger.

'I don't think it's a bad business,' said Mrs Pepperpot.

'I shall have a terrible time. The whole town will laugh when they see I have a wife the size of a pepperpot.'

'Who cares?' she answered. 'That doesn't matter a bit. Now put me down on the floor so that I can get ready to go to the grocer and buy your macaroni.'

But her husband wouldn't hear of her going; he would go to the grocer himself.

'That'll be a lot of use!' she said. 'When you get home you'll have forgotten to buy the macaroni. I'm sure even if I wrote "macaroni" right across your forehead you'd bring back cinnamon and salt herrings instead.'

'But how are you going to walk all that way with those tiny legs?'

'Put me in your coat pocket; then I won't need to walk.'

There was no help for it, so Mr Pepperpot put his wife in his pocket and set off for the shop.

Soon she started talking: 'My goodness me, what a lot of strange things you have in your pocket – screws and nails, tobacco and matches – there's even a fish-hook! You'll have to take that out at once; I might get it caught in my skirt.'

'Don't talk so loud,' said her husband as he took out the fish-hook. 'We're going into the shop now.'

It was an old-fashioned village store where they sold everything from prunes to coffee cups. The grocer was particularly proud of the coffee cups and held one up for Mr Pepperpot to see. This made his wife curious and she popped her head out of his pocket.

'You stay where you are!' whispered Mr Pepperpot.

'I beg your pardon, did you say anything?' asked the grocer.

'No, no, I was just humming a little tune,' said Mr Pepperpot. 'Tra-la-la!'

'What colour are the cups?' whispered his wife. And her husband sang:

> '*The cups are blue*
> *With gold edge too,*
> *But they cost too much*
> *So that won't do!*'

After that Mrs Pepperpot kept quiet – but not for long. When her husband pulled out his tobacco tin she couldn't resist hanging on to the lid. Neither her husband nor anyone else in the shop noticed her slipping on to

144

the counter and hiding behind a flour-bag.
From there she darted silently across to the
scales, crawled under them, past a pair of
kippers wrapped in newspaper, and found
herself next to the coffee cups.

'Aren't they pretty!' she whispered, and
took a step backwards to get a better view.
Whoops! She fell right into the macaroni

145

drawer which had been left open. She hastily covered herself up with macaroni, but the grocer heard the scratching noise and quickly banged the drawer shut. You see, it did sometimes happen that mice got in the drawers, and that's not the sort of thing you want people to know about, so the grocer pretended nothing had happened and went on serving.

cer had mistaken his wife for a mouse. So he took the cups and rushed home as fast as he could. By the time he got there he was in a sweat of fear that his wife might have been squeezed to death in the macaroni bag.

'Oh, my dear wife,' he muttered to himself. 'My poor darling wife. I'll never again be ashamed of you being the size of a pepperpot – as long as you're still alive!'

When he opened the door she was standing by the cooking-stove, dishing up the macaroni – as large as life; in fact, as large as you or I.

This story is by Alf Prøysen

How the Cat Became

Things were running very smoothly and most of the creatures were highly pleased with themselves. Lion was already famous. Even the little shrews and moles and spiders were pretty well known.

But among all these busy creatures there was one who seemed to be getting nowhere. It was Cat.

Cat was a real oddity. The others didn't know what to make of him at all.

He lived in a hollow tree in the wood. Every night, when the rest of the creatures were sound asleep, he retired to the depths of his tree – then such sounds, such screechings, yowlings, wailings! The bats that slept upside-down all day long in the hollows of the tree branches awoke with a start and fled with their wing-tips stuffed into their ears. It seemed to them that Cat was having the worst nightmares ever – ten at a time.

But no. Cat was tuning his violin.

If only you could have seen him! Curled in

the warm smooth hollow of his tree, gazing up through the hole at the top of the trunk, smiling at the stars, winking at the moon – his violin tucked under his chin. Ah, Cat was a happy one.

And all night long he sat there composing his tunes.

Now the creatures didn't like this at all. They saw no use in his music, it made no food, it built no nest, it didn't even keep him warm. And the way Cat lounged around all day, sleeping in the sun, was just more than they could stand.

'He's a bad example,' said Beaver, 'he never does a stroke of work! What if our children think they can live as idly as he does?'

'It's time,' said Weasel, 'that Cat had a job like everybody else in the world.'

So the creatures of the wood formed a Committee to persuade Cat to take a job.

Jay, Magpie, and Parrot went along at dawn and sat in the topmost twigs of Cat's old tree. As soon as Cat poked his head out, they all began together:

'You've to get a job. Get a job! Get a job!'

That was only the beginning of it. All day long, everywhere he went, those birds were at him:

'Get a job! Get a job!'

And try as he would, Cat could not get a wink of sleep.

That night he went back to his tree early.

154

He was far too tired to practise on his violin and fell fast asleep in a few minutes. Next morning, when he poked his head out of the tree at first light, the three birds of the Committee were there again, loud as ever:

'Get a job!'

Cat ducked back down into his tree and began to think. He wasn't going to start grubbing around in the wet woods all day, as they wanted him to. Oh no. He wouldn't have any time to play his violin if he did that. There was only one thing to do and he did it.

He tucked his violin under his arm and suddenly jumped out at the top of the tree and set off through the woods at a run. Behind him, shouting and calling, came Jay, Magpie, and Parrot.

Other creatures that were about their daily work in the undergrowth looked up when Cat ran past. No one had ever seen Cat run before.

'Cat's up to something,' they called to each other. 'Maybe he's going to get a job at last.'

Deer, Wild Boar, Bear, Ferret, Mongoose,

Porcupine, and a cloud of birds set off after Cat to see where he was going.

After a great deal of running they came to the edge of the forest. There they stopped. As they peered through the leaves they looked sideways at each other and trembled. Ahead of them, across an open field covered with haycocks, was Man's farm.

But Cat wasn't afraid. He went straight on, over the field, and up to Man's door. He raised his paw and banged as hard as he could in the middle of the door.

Man was so surprised to see Cat that at first he just stood, eyes wide, mouth open. No creature ever dared to come on to his fields, let alone knock at his door. Cat spoke first.

'I've come for a job,' he said.

'A job?' asked Man, hardly able to believe his ears.

'Work,' said Cat. 'I want to earn my living.'

Man looked him up and down, then saw his long claws.

'You look as if you'd make a fine rat-catcher,' said Man.

Cat was surprised to hear that. He wondered what it was about him that made him
look like a rat-catcher. Still, he wasn't going
to miss the chance of a job. So he stuck out
his chest and said: 'Been doing it for years.'

'Well then, I've a job for you,' said Man.
'My farm's swarming with rats and mice.
They're in my haystacks, they're in my corn
sacks, and they're all over the pantry.'

So before Cat knew where he was, he had
been signed on as a Rat-and-Mouse-Catcher.
His pay was milk, and meat, and a place at
the fireside. He slept all day and worked all
night.

At first he had a terrible time. The rats
pulled his tail, the mice nipped his ears. They
climbed on to rafters above him and dropped
down – thump! on to him in the dark. They
teased the life out of him.

But Cat was a quick learner. At the end
of the week he could lay out a dozen rats and
twice as many mice within half an hour. If
he'd gone on laying them out all night there
would pretty soon have been none left, and
Cat would have been out of a job. So he
just caught a few each night – in the first ten

157

minutes or so. Then he retired into the barn and played his violin till morning. This was just the job he had been looking for.

Man was delighted with him. And Mrs Man thought he was beautiful. She took him on to her lap and stroked him for hours on end. What a life! thought Cat. If only those silly creatures in the dripping wet woods could see him now!

Well, when the other farmers saw what a fine rat-and-mouse-catcher Cat was, they all wanted cats too. Soon there were so many cats that our Cat decided to form a string band. Oh yes, they were all great violinists. Every night, after making one pile of rats and another of mice, each cat left his farm and was away over the fields to a little dark spinney.

Then what tunes! All night long . . .

Pretty soon lady cats began to arrive. Now, every night, instead of just music, there was dancing too. And what dances! If only you could have crept up there and peeped into the glade from behind a tree and seen the cats dancing – the glossy furred ladies and the tomcats, some pearly grey, some ginger red, and all with wonderful green flashing eyes. Up and down the glade, with the music flying out all over the night.

At dawn they hung their violins in the larch trees, dashed back to the farms, and pretended they had been working all night among the rats and mice. They lapped their milk hungrily, stretched out at the fireside, and fell asleep with smiles on their faces.

This story is by Ted Hughes

J. Roodie

J. Roodie was wild and bad, although he was only nine. Nobody owned him, so he lived in a creek bed with his animals, who had nasty names. His dog was called Grip, which was what it did to passers-by. He had a bad-tempered brumby called Kick, and a raggedy crow called Pincher. Pincher swooped down and stole kids' twenty cents worth of chips when they came out of the fish and chip shop. J. Roodie had trained him to do that.

Nobody ever went for a stroll along the creek, because they knew better. J. Roodie kept a supply of dried cow manure and used it as ammunition, because he didn't have pleasant manners at all. He never had a bath and

161

his fingernails were a disgrace and a shame.

There was a cottage near the creek with a FOR SALE notice, but no one wanted to live near J. Roodie. Everyone muttered, 'Someone should do something about that awful J. Roodie!' but nobody knew what to do and they were too scared to get close enough to do it, anyhow.

J. Roodie painted creek mud scars across his face, and blacked out his front teeth. He drew biro tattoos over his back and he stuck a metal ring with a piece missing through his nose so that it looked pierced. He swaggered around town and pulled faces at babies in prams and made them bawl, and he filled the kindergarten sandpit with quicksand. Luckily the teacher discovered it before she lost any pupils.

He let Grip scare everyone they met, and he let Kick eat people's prize roses, and he was just as much a nuisance going out of town as he was going in. But nobody came and told him off, because they were all nervous of tough J. Roodie and his wild animals.

One day he was annoyed to see that the

FOR SALE notice had been removed from the cottage and someone had moved in. He sent Grip over to scare them away.

Grip bared his fangs and slobbered like a hungry wolf at the little old lady who had just moved in.

'Oh, what a sweet puppy!' said the little old lady whose name was Miss Daisy
Thrimble. Grip had never been called 'sweet'
before, so he stopped slobbering and wagged
his tail. Miss Daisy Thrimble gave him a
bath and fluffed up his coat with a hair dryer.
'I'll call you Curly,' she said. 'Here's a nice
mat for you, Curly.'

Grip felt self-conscious about going back
to J. Roodie with his coat all in little ringlets,
and besides, the mat was cosier than a creek
bed, so he went to sleep.

J. Roodie waited two days for him and then he sent Pincher to the cottage. Miss Daisy was hanging out washing. 'Caaaaawwwrk!' Pincher croaked horribly, flapping his big, raggedy, untidy wings and snapping his beak.

'What a poor little lost bird,' said Miss Daisy. She plucked Pincher out of the sky and carried him inside. She filled a saucer with canary seed and fetched a mirror and a bell. 'I'll call you Pretty Boy,' she said. 'And I'll teach you how to talk.'

Pincher already knew some not very nice words that J. Roodie taught him, but Miss Daisy Thrimble looked so sweet-faced and well-behaved that Pincher didn't say them. He tapped the bell with his beak, and looked in the little mirror, and decided that it was very nice to have playthings.

J. Roodie grew tired of waiting for Pincher, and he sent Kick to scare Miss Daisy away. Kick pawed the lawn and carried on like a rodeo and rolled his eyes till the whites showed.

'Oh, what a darling little Shetland pony!' said Miss Daisy. She caught Kick and brushed away the creek mud and plaited his mane into rosettes tied up with red ribbons. 'There's a cart in the shed,' she said. 'You can help me do the shopping. I'll call you Twinkle.'

Kick snorted indignantly, but then he saw his reflection in a kitchen window and was amazed that he could look so dignified. He stopped worrying about his new name when Miss Daisy brought him a handful of oats.

J. Roodie marched over to the cottage and yelled, 'YAAAAH!' at the top of his voice. He jumped up and down and brandished a spear and rattled some coconuts with faces painted on them, which were tied to his belt. They looked just like shrunken heads. 'WHEEEEEE!' yelled J. Roodie. 'GRRRRRRR!'

'What a dear little high-spirited boy!' said Miss Daisy. 'But you certainly need a bath.' She dumped J. Roodie into a tub and when she had finished scrubbing, he was as clean and sweet-smelling as an orange. Miss Daisy dressed him in a blue checked shirt and nice clean pants and brushed his hair. 'There,' she said. 'I shall call you Joe. I'll be proud to take you into town with me in my little cart.'

She sat Joe Roodie next to her, and Kick, called Twinkle now, trotted smartly into town, and Grip, called Curly now, ran beside and didn't nip anyone they met.

People said, 'Good morning, Miss Daisy. Is that your little nephew?'

'His name is Joe,' Miss Daisy said proudly. 'I think he lived in the creek bed before he came to stay with me.'

'He can't have,' they said. 'J. Roodie lives in the creek bed and he'd never let anyone else live there.'

'J. who?' asked Miss Daisy, because she was rather hard of hearing. 'Do you know anyone called J. something or other, Joe?'

Joe Roodie didn't answer right away. He'd just felt in the pockets of his new pants and found a pocket knife with six blades, and a ball of red twine, and some interesting rusty keys, and eleven marbles.

'We'll buy some apples and make a pie for our supper,' said Miss Daisy. 'Maybe we could invite that J. boy they said lives in the creek. What do you think, Joe?'

Joe Roodie hadn't tasted apple pie for as many years as he hadn't had a bath, and his mouth watered.

'There used to be a kid called J. Roodie in the creek bed,' he said. 'But he doesn't live there any more.'

This story is by Robin Klein

Uninvited Ghosts

Marian and Simon were sent to bed early on the day that the Brown family moved house. By then everyone had lost their temper with everyone else; the cat had been sick on the sitting-room carpet; the dog had run away twice. If you have ever moved you will know what kind of a day it had been. Packing cases and newspaper all over the place . . . sandwiches instead of proper meals . . . the kettle lost and a wardrobe stuck on the stairs and Mrs Brown's favourite vase broken. There was bread and baked beans for supper, the television wouldn't work and the water wasn't hot so when all was said and done the children didn't object too violently to being packed off to bed.

They'd had enough, too. They had one last argument about who was going to sleep by the window, put on their pyjamas, got into bed, switched the lights out . . . and it was at that point that the ghost came out of the bottom drawer of the chest of drawers.

It oozed out, a grey cloudy shape about three feet long smelling faintly of woodsmoke, sat down on a chair and began to hum to itself. It looked like a bundle of bedclothes, except that it was not solid: you could see, quite clearly, the cushion on the chair beneath it.

Marian gave a shriek. 'That's a ghost!'

'Oh, be quiet, dear, do,' said the ghost. 'That noise goes right through my head. And it's not nice to call people names.' It took out a ball of wool and some needles and began to knit.

What would you have done? Well, yes – Simon and Marian did just that and I dare say you can imagine what happened. You try telling your mother that you can't get to sleep because there's a ghost sitting in the room clacking its knitting-needles and humming. Mrs Brown said the kind of things she could be expected to say and the ghost continued sitting there knitting and humming and Mrs Brown went out, banging the door and saying threatening things about if there's so much as another word from either of you . . .

'She can't see it,' said Marian to Simon.

' 'Course not, dear,' said the ghost. 'It's the kiddies I'm here for. Love kiddies, I do. We're going to be ever such friends.'

'Go away!' yelled Simon. 'This is our house now!'

'No it isn't,' said the ghost smugly. 'Always been here, I have. A hundred years and more. Seen plenty of families come and go, I have. Go to bye-byes now, there's good children.'

The children glared at it and buried themselves under the bedclothes. And, eventually, slept.

The next night it was there again. This time it was smoking a long white pipe and reading a newspaper dated 1842. Beside it was a second grey cloudy shape. 'Hello, dearies,' said the ghost. 'Say how do you do to my Auntie Edna.'

'She can't come here too,' wailed Marian.

'Oh yes she can,' said the ghost. 'Always comes here in August, does Auntie. She likes a change.'

Auntie Edna was even worse, if possible. She sucked peppermint drops that smelled so strong that Mrs Brown, when she came to kiss the children good night, looked suspiciously under their pillows. She also sang hymns in a loud squeaky voice. The children lay there groaning and the ghosts sang and rustled the newspapers and ate peppermints.

The next night there were three of them. 'Meet Uncle Charlie!' said the first ghost. The children groaned.

'And Jip,' said the ghost. 'Here, Jip, good dog – come and say hello to the kiddies, then.' A large grey dog that you could see straight through came out from under the bed, wagging its tail. The cat, who had been curled up beside Marian's feet (it was supposed to sleep in the kitchen, but there are always ways for a resourceful cat to get what it wants), gave a howl and shot on top of the wardrobe, where it sat spitting. The dog lay down in the middle of the rug and set about scratching itself vigorously; evidently it had ghost fleas, too.

Uncle Charlie was unbearable. He had a loud cough that kept going off like a machine-gun and he told the longest most pointless stories the children had ever heard. He said he too loved kiddies and he knew kiddies loved stories. In the middle of the seventh story the children went to sleep out of sheer boredom.

The following week the ghosts left the bedroom and were to be found all over the house. The children had no peace at all. They'd be quietly doing their homework and all of a sudden Auntie Edna would be breathing down their necks reciting arithmetic tables. The original ghost took to sitting on top of the television with his legs in front of the picture. Uncle Charlie told his stories all through the best programmes and the dog lay permanently at the top of the stairs. The Browns' cat became quite hysterical, refused to eat and went to live on the top shelf of the kitchen dresser.

Something had to be done. Marian and Simon also were beginning to show the effects; their mother decided they looked peaky and bought an appalling sticky brown vitamin medicine from the chemists to strengthen them. 'It's the ghosts!' wailed the children. 'We don't need vitamins!' Their mother said severely that she didn't want to hear another word of this silly nonsense about ghosts. Auntie Edna, who was sitting smirking on the other side of the kitchen table at that very moment, nodded vigorously and took out a packet of humbugs which she sucked noisily.

'We've got to get them to go and live somewhere else,' said Marian. But where, that was the problem, and how? It was then that they had a bright idea. On Sunday the Browns were all going to see their uncle who was rather rich and lived alone in a big house with thick carpets everywhere and empty rooms and the biggest colour television you ever saw. Plenty of room for ghosts.

They were very cunning. They suggested to the ghosts that they might like a drive in the country. The ghosts said at first that they were quite comfortable where they were, thank you, and they didn't fancy these new-fangled motor-cars, not at their time of life. But then Auntie Edna remembered that she liked looking at the pretty flowers and the trees and finally they agreed to give it a try. They sat in a row on the back shelf of the car. Mrs Brown kept asking why there was such a strong smell of peppermint and Mr Brown kept roaring at Simon and Marian to keep still while he was driving. The fact was that the ghosts were shoving them; it was like being nudged by three cold damp flannels. And the ghost dog, who had come along too of course, was car-sick.

When they got to Uncle Dick's the ghosts came in and had a look round. They liked the expensive carpets and the enormous television. They slid in and out of the wardrobes and walked through the doors and the walls and sent Uncle Dick's budgerigars into a decline from which they have never recovered. Nice place, they said, nice and comfy.

'Why not stay here?' said Simon, in an offhand tone.

'Couldn't do that,' said the ghosts firmly. 'No kiddies. Dull. We like a place with a bit of life to it.' And they piled back into the car and sang hymns all the way home to the Browns' house. They also ate toast. There were real toast-crumbs on the floor and the children got the blame.

Simon and Marian were in despair. The ruder they were to the ghosts the more the ghosts liked it. 'Cheeky!' they said indulgently. 'What a cheeky little pair of kiddies! There now . . . come and give uncle a kiss.' The children weren't even safe in the bath. One or other of the ghosts would come and sit on the taps and talk to them. Uncle Charlie had produced a mouth organ and played the same tune over and over again; it was quite excruciating. The children went around with their hands over their ears. Mrs Brown took them to the doctor to find out if there was something wrong with their hearing. The children knew better than to say anything to the doctor about the ghosts. It was pointless saying anything to anyone.

I don't know what would have happened if Mrs Brown hadn't happened to

176

make friends with Mrs Walker from down the road. Mrs Walker had twin babies, and one day she brought the babies along for tea.

Now one baby is bad enough. Two babies are trouble in a big way. These babies created pandemonium. When they weren't both howling they were crawling around the floor pulling the tablecloths off the tables or hitting their heads on the chairs and hauling the books out of the bookcases. They threw their food all over the kitchen and flung cups of milk on the floor. Their mother mopped up after them and every time she tried to have a conversation with Mrs Brown the babies bawled in chorus so that no one could hear a word.

In the middle of this the ghosts appeared. One baby was yelling its head off and the other was glueing pieces of chewed up bread on to the front of the television. The ghosts swooped down on them with happy cries. 'Oh!' they trilled. 'Bless their little hearts then, diddums, give auntie a smile then.' And the babies stopped in mid-howl and gazed at the ghosts. The ghosts cooed at the babies and the babies cooed at the ghosts.

The ghosts chattered to the babies and sang them songs and the babies chattered back and were as good as gold for the next hour and their mother had the first proper conversation she'd had in weeks. When they went the ghosts stood in a row at the window, waving.

Simon and Marian knew when to seize an opportunity. That evening they had a talk with the ghosts. At first the ghosts raised objections. They didn't fancy the idea of moving, they said; you got set in your ways, at their age; Auntie Edna reckoned a strange house would be the death of her.

The children talked about the babies, relentlessly.

And the next day they led the ghosts down the road, followed by the ghost dog, and into the Walkers' house. Mrs Walker doesn't know to this day why the babies, who had been screaming for the last half hour, suddenly stopped and broke into great smiles. And she has never understood why, from that day forth, the babies became the most tranquil, quiet, amiable babies in the area. The ghosts kept the babies amused from morning to night. The babies thrived; the ghosts were happy; the ghost dog, who was actually a bitch, settled down so well that she had puppies which is one of the most surprising aspects of the whole business. The Brown children heaved a sigh of relief and got back to normal life. The babies, though, I have to tell you, grew up somewhat peculiar.

This story is by Penelope Lively

A BARREL OF STORIES FOR SEVEN YEAR OLDS
Collected by PAT THOMSON

Roll out the barrel and discover . . . naughty Angela and her sticky school trick; Frankel, the farmer who outwits the Czar; Ignatius Binz, a boy with a truly magnificent nose; a Hallowe'en trick that goes wrong; and a whole host of other wonderful characters and stories. You won't want to stop reading until you get right to the bottom of the barrel!

The latest terrific title in a series of story collections from children's book specialist Pat Thomson.

'Lively and rich collections of stories for all ages'
Books for Keeps

0 552 52817 X

A SACKFUL OF STORIES FOR
EIGHT YEAR OLDS
Collected by PAT THOMSON

Delve into this sack of stories and you will find . . . a Martian wearing Granny's jumper, that well-known comic fairy-tale pair Handsel and Gristle, a unicorn, a leprechaun, a princess who is a pig, and many other strange and exciting characters. You won't want to stop reading until you get right to the bottom of the sack!

'There are thirteen stories to a sackful and each and every one is a tried-and-tested cracker'
The Sunday Telegraph

'Will be enjoyed by children of all ages'
The Times Educational Supplement

'Will stimulate even the most reluctant reader'
Junior Education

Read Alone or Read Aloud

0 552 527300